EGMONT PRESS: ETHICAL PUBLISHING

Egmont Press is about turning writers into successful authors and children into passionate readers – producing books that enrich and entertain. As a responsible children's publisher, we go even further, considering the world in which our consumers are growing up.

Safety First
Naturally, all of our books meet legal safety requirements. But we go further than this; every book with play value is tested to the highest standards – if it fails, it's back to the drawing-board.

Made Fairly
We are working to ensure that the workers involved in our supply chain – the people that make our books – are treated with fairness and respect.

Responsible Forestry
We are committed to ensuring all our papers come from environmentally and socially responsible forest sources.

For more information, please visit our website at
www.egmont.co.uk/ethicalpublishing

For Paul

EGMONT
We bring stories to life

Published in Great Britain 2006
by Egmont UK Limited
239 Kensington High Street, London W8 6SA

Text copyright © 2006 N. S. Narayan

The moral rights of the author have been asserted

ISBN 978 1 4052 1878 8
ISBN 1 4052 1878 9

1 3 5 7 9 10 8 6 4 2

A CIP catalogue record for this title is available
from the British Library

Typeset by Avon DataSet Ltd, Bidford on Avon
Printed and bound in Great Britain by the CPI Group

THE PARADISE PLOT

WINSTON

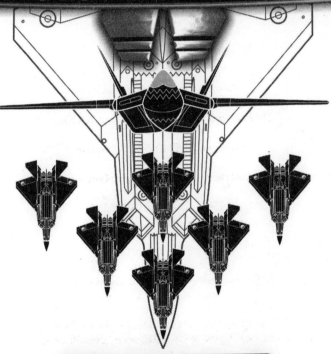

N. S. NARAYAN

EGMONT

Prologue

PARADISE LOST

Paradise Island, Atlantic Ocean

The sun looped over Paradise Island, plopping into the Atlantic Ocean like a fiery football. 7,122 miles away, in a hideout hewn from volcanic rock, someone with glowing white hair typed a single word on to a laptop: 'GO'. At once a huge black shape loomed out of the Atlantic, parting the waters before it. Seagulls fled screeching at its approach. The sheep grazing on a hillside above the beach on Paradise Island took one look at the monster and ran.

In a nearby farmhouse eleven-year-old Lucy Carter was in the middle of dinner with her mum, Mary, her dad, Hank, and her six-year-old brother, Brad. Dinner was mutton stew. Again. Lucy had been chewing away at the same hunk for five minutes. It sat in her mouth like a wad of stale gum.

'Pops, can I get up from the table? I need to go pee.'

'Sure.' Hank nodded.

Lucy felt guilty for a split millisecond. Did Dad know? If he did, he wouldn't say anything. He was soft like that.

'I hate mutton, Daddeee. Makes me wanna puke,' Lucy heard Brad whining.

'Brad!' snapped Mum.

Then came Dad's patient voice. 'You eat your mutton, kiddo. You wanna be a big guy, doncha?'

In the bathroom Lucy took the mutton out of her mouth, added the bits she had hidden in her pocket, wrapped the lot in toilet paper and flushed it away.

Everything was unusually quiet as she padded back to the kitchen, but Lucy didn't notice. She was dreaming of Big Macs and chicken tacos, Hershey Bars and Oreos. Anything but mutton. Her mother's piercing scream shattered the silence. 'Uh-oh,' Lucy thought. 'Brad's in trouble.' Her little brother just wasn't sneaky enough. That was his problem. But it wasn't quite that simple. Lucy arrived at the kitchen door to find four men dressed in black leather diving suits and masks. Her mother and Brad were tied to their chairs, their mouths gagged. Hank was slung over one of the men's shoulders like a leg of lamb. A plate fell from the dinner table and shattered. Lucy was jerked out of her trance. As silent as a moving shadow, she slipped into the corridor, took Dad's mobile from his coat and ran out into the night.

She turned on the mobile and keyed in a number with trembling hands. Uncle Joe was a policeman. 'It's me, Lucy,' she hissed. 'Please. It's Dad. I need your help.' But with a sick feeling she heard a voice telling her there was no credit left on the mobile.

The men came out, the largest of the group still carrying Dad over his shoulders. They chucked him in the back of a green Jeep and revved the engine.

Lucy decided to follow on her bike. Her feet worked furiously, but it was no good. She couldn't keep up. The Jeep slipped out of sight. Now she was pedalling like a maniac, following the rumble of the vehicle. The salty wind lashed her, the spume from the sea stung her face. Her head was hot. Who would want to kidnap Dad? He was just a sheep farmer – had been ever since he quit being a lawyer in New York five years ago. He had no enemies . . .

The engine of the Jeep suddenly died. The kidnappers had gone less than a mile. Lucy was sweaty and breathless when she came to a stop. She left her bike by the roadside and clambered up the rocks to get a better view. The Jeep was parked on Penguin Beach, next to a small harbour. Lucy crept in close. She could see tall purple flames shooting straight up from a pile of rocks. Over it all hung a smell: bittersweet and sickly, of almonds and sugar. Lucy shivered. Who were these men? What were they doing? Why did they want her dad? Fear made her heart hammer and her legs shake. She fell to the ground.

The men were chattering away, as if kidnap was just part of a normal day's work.

'Easy with that guy, the bald one shouted.' 'Hope will want the goods in one piece.'

'Keep your hair on,' answered the big man as he dragged Dad out of the Jeep.

Lucy was so close she could see the diamonds that glittered in his teeth. They spelled out the words L-O-V-E and H-A-T-E. Lucy willed her father to do something. Dad was the strongest man she knew. Why wasn't he fighting back? Then he opened his eyes. Looked straight at her. Lucy thought she was going to scream. But she didn't. Dad didn't make a sound to betray that he had seen her. He only closed his eyes again.

The muttered put-put-put of a speedboat started up. The men went down to the harbour. They loaded Dad on to the speedboat. It pulled out, heading for a vast, shadowy shape floating in the water. In a gleam of moonlight Lucy saw the men scaling the sides of the thing. Then they vanished inside it.

Lucy stood on the beach watching the black shape sink into the sea. Dad had been swallowed by a submarine.

CHAPTER ONE

Duffham Hall, Berkshire, UK

'WHAT THE –!' Roger Smee, headmaster of Duffham Hall, looked down at the boy who had the nerve to disturb him on Sunday afternoon. 'Weally, of all the cheek!' Smee had just lunched on five slices of roast beef, three Yorkshire puddings and two helpings of trifle. He was sinking into a stupor when he was roused by a loud banging at the door.

'I'm Winston Wright.' A very short boy on the doorstep held out his hand. He was one of the most peculiar creatures Smee had ever seen. Huge black eyes in a skinny face, like a cartoon alien. 'This is the BBC. They're covering the story,' the boy continued, casually indicating the three men behind him.

'What stowy?' headmaster Smee asked, bewildered. 'Wepeat your name. You're not one of my lot, are you?'

Somehow the youngster was already in Smee's private sitting room, a feat not one of his 865 pupils had ever managed, and firing out instructions to the camera crew.

'If I go here,' said the boy, settling into Smee's favourite leather armchair, 'you'll get a good view of the tennis courts and the swimming pools. I think that strikes the right note, don't you?'

'Yeah, that'll work,' grunted the cameraman.

'What did you say your name was?' Smee asked the boy again.

'Winston Wright,' said Winston. 'Headmaster, if you'll take that seat the camera will get a good view of your cosy room.'

'But what the blazes are you doing here?' Without realising it, Smee sat down in the chair Winston had pointed to. 'What are these people doing?'

'Who, the TV people?' said Winston casually. 'They're doing a story on me, as it happens.' He turned to the cameraman and added, 'Let us know when you're ready to roll.'

'But who are *you*?' Smee was becoming exasperated.

'They liked the angle,' Winston went on, as if he hadn't heard Smee's interruption. 'Posh school refuses scholarship to dinner lady's son. That sort of thing.'

A light bulb went on in Smee's head. He had been trying for months to get the BBC's *Look West* to do a piece on Duffham Hall. He wanted to show how Britain's oldest and richest school was opening its arms to 'the under-pwivileged'.

'Is that what this is about? Are you one of the scholarship candidates?'

Winston smiled. 'Not just *one* of the scholarship candidates. I got 99 per cent in English and 99.5 per cent in General Knowledge. The highest scores ever, I believe.'

Winston's general knowledge began where Google's left off. It was hard for him sometimes to be patient with those of normal intelligence. Smee remembered the case clearly now. A twelve-year-old boy had sat the scholarship exam for Duffham Hall. By some extraordinary fluke he'd received outstanding scores in all the papers except maths.

'You couldn't add up,' Smee protested.

Winston frowned. 'I've never believed in wasting mental energy on mechanical tasks. I cracked arithmetic when I was four. Now I generally use a calculator . . . Are you aware of my circumstances?'

'Er, no,' said Smee reluctantly. He didn't want to enter into a debate with this strange child.

But when he got going Winston was an irresistible force. Smee discovered it was he who was the movable object. Most other adults found themselves in a similar position with the prodigy.

'My mum brought us up, me and my sister, Gemma, without help from anybody. She worked three jobs to make sure we had everything we needed.'

'What happened to your dad?' Smee asked, curious despite of himself.

'Never mind about him,' said Winston shortly. 'My mum's the star. She works as a cleaner. And a school dinner lady. Not at a posh school like this.' Winston gestured to the grounds, which boasted acres of playing fields, fourteen tennis courts and two Olympic-sized swimming pools. 'An ordinary school.'

'Er,' the headmaster began, but . . . Winston cut him short.

'Most of your scholarship candidates have extra help, private tutors, special courses. Not me.'

Winston neglected to add that he could have paid the school fees himself. Unknown to his mum, he'd first invested his pocket money in the oil futures market two years ago. Winston had reasoned correctly that energy shortages were reaching crisis point. As petrol rationing was introduced and people shivered through winter, unable to afford to heat their houses, Winston prospered. His nest egg currently stood at £156,077. His mum was always pleasantly surprised to find that her wages went a lot further than she'd have thought possible. Winston was the only one who knew why.

Smee had taken an instant dislike to this egotistical brat. 'And you want to join Duffham Hall? You're weally TOO YOUNG, sonny. What are you – twelve? Duffham boys start when they're thirteen. We can't have you in a class of thirteen-year-olds. You won't fit in.'

Winston fixed the headmaster with a black stare that pierced him like a sharpened knitting needle.

'Would you mind repeating that last bit, headmaster? The lights just blew,' the cameraman intervened.

'But I didn't know that the camewa –' Smee spluttered.

Winston cut him off again. 'Too young? It's illegal to discriminate against women. But you're shutting the door on me because I'm too young!' Turning to the crew, he added cheerfully, 'Did you get all that?'

The cameraman nodded.

Smee had not become headmaster without being able to think – sometimes. He turned to the camera with a smile that made his face ache. 'Duffham Hall has opened its doors to a wemarkable young boy,' he announced, beaming. 'He is from a modest background. But he is unusually gifted. He is just the sort of boy we would like to have in this twenty-first-centuwy school. Therefore I am offering Winston Wight a totally fwee place at this histowic school – all his expenses will be met by Duffham's funds as well.'

It was a slow news day and the piece on Winston got five minutes on *Look West's* evening bulletin. There were shots of him strolling around the grounds with Smee, taking a dip in one of the enormous pools, having his first riding lesson. Winston watched the story in the Wrights' front room, with his fifteen-year-old sister, Gemma, and his mum, Shirley. The family snacked on Potato Smiles, leftovers from mum's job at Utminister School.

Gemma was sick of Winston getting all the attention. 'Duffham's not for us. It's full of snobs. Those boys have chauffeurs to take them to school and nannies to wipe their bums.'

Mum's feelings ran deeper. She was dismayed. And a bit frightened. She didn't want to lose her little boy. She didn't want Winston to go off to this fancy school and come back with stiff new clothes and a funny accent. 'But why, Winnie? I don't understand *why* you want to go to boarding school.'

Winston swallowed. He couldn't tell Mum the real reason. That he didn't want to end up as a wage slave like *her*. Bossed around all day. *Powerless*. 'Um, you're always telling me to stop staring at the computer screen and go out to play. They've got fantastic sports fields,' he said.

His mum was unconvinced. She tried to hold back a sob. 'I'll never see you.'

'Mum! They have really long holidays at Duffham Hall.' Winston put his arm round her shoulder. 'You'll see more of me than you want to.'

'I'll miss you, Winnie.'

'Um . . . I'll miss you too, Mum.'

Actually, Winston was starting to miss his mum already, though he didn't want to admit it, even to himself. Duffham hadn't seemed a very friendly place. Still, he wouldn't be there for ever. Duffham Hall was only a stepping stone. [A platform to his dreams.]

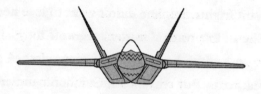

CHAPTER TWO

'Master Wight,' the headmaster snapped.

'Sir,' Winston answered politely, dragging his eyes away from the window and his thoughts away from what he'd do once he left Duffham. Prime Minister, he quite fancied being Prime Minister of Great Britain.

'I will not have students day-dweaming. It is wude. Tell us what Wudyard Kipling's poem "If" is about.'

'Yes, sir,' Winston replied. '"If" consists of advice to boys on how to be the leaders of tomorrow. The poem is almost a shopping list of the qualities a leader needs. Kipling thinks the courage to stand up for what is right, even if everyone is against you, is one of the most important leadership qualities.'

'Hmm,' the headmaster murmured, baffled.

Winston smiled, thankful that he'd had plenty of

practice at multi-tasking. Five per cent of his mind had been on Smee's droning lesson while the rest got on with more important matters. Several boys in the class were smirking at the head's discomfort. A giggle escaped from a boy called Toby Smith. Smee pounced.

'What's so funny, Smith?'

'Er . . . nothing, sir.'

'Extwa detention. That's what funny. You can start by unblocking the staff toilet. I noticed a nasty smell coming from it.'

'Yes, sir,' stuttered Toby miserably.

'I want that toilet SPOTLESS. So clean, Smith, that you could eat your lunch off it.' Smee beamed. 'That's an idea. Who wants Smith to eat his lunch out of the toilet?'

'Me, sir,' chorused those in the class who always sucked up to the headmaster. The others looked at the ground, too scared to breathe.

Winston couldn't stop himself. 'I don't,' he said.

'What?!'

'I'm just thinking of Duffham's reputation, sir. If Toby gets worms, his parents might sue.'

'Not funny, Wight. Double detention, now. You can start by helping Toby clean the toilet.'

Toby and Winston left the room in silence,

laughter echoing in their ears. While Toby went straight to the toilet, Winston took a detour. He found Toby a few minutes later, holding a filthy toilet brush.

'It's foul,' Toby moaned.

Winston took one look at the lumpy brush and overflowing loo. 'Don't bother with that,' he advised. He had rooted around in the broom cupboard and found a packet of Draxo – the miracle unblocker. 'Let's just chuck some of this in and leave it. Come back in ten minutes and flush. It'll work wonders.'

'But –' Toby stared at Winston, horrified. 'What if Smee catches us?'

'He won't. Let's go. I want to catch the news.'

Winston ambled down the hall to the common room and turned on the TV, secure in the knowledge that Smee loved the sound of his own voice too much to leave class early.

The energy crisis was getting worse. In California fourteen people had been taken to hospital with gunshot wounds after a man – fed up with standing for two hours in a petrol queue – went berserk with a handgun. In Paris burglars had broken into the main government fuel warehouse and stolen 20,000 gallons of petrol. The city had ground to a standstill as a result, with millions of people stranded without lights and power. There were reports of piracy on the North Sea. A giant BritOil tanker had vanished without a trace.

The energy news came to an end and a motherly woman with frizzy brown hair and dangly earrings came on screen. Mystic Marge. 'I've got a special treat for viewers today,' Marge promised. 'We're going to remote Paradise Island, 300 miles from the coast of America in the Atlantic Ocean. Paradise land of magic and mystery. We'll –'

Winston flicked the TV off and drew an envelope out of his pocket. He was sick of the mumbo-jumbo that TV had started to spout. Maybe it was the uncertainty of the energy crisis that made people leap on every crazy bandwagon going. He began jotting down some thoughts on the thick, creamy paper. He had found a packet of fancy stationery on the floor and helped himself to an envelope. Not stealing so much as a redistribution of resources. He was so engrossed in plotting his future – school president, then one day Prime Minister – that half an hour must have passed.

'Yo! GOOGLE!' a voice bellowed behind him.

Winston stuffed the envelope into his pocket, sighing. It hadn't taken the Duffham bullies long to spot there was something different about Winston. His protruding eyes and gangly neck. Not to mention the way his mind operated at warp speed. Still, he could have wished they'd been more inventive in their choice of nickname than going for an Internet search engine.

'I said GOOGLE!' Julian Tut-Tut was sidekick to Jago Lushington – the biggest bully in the school. 'You've done it this time,' Julian boomed. 'The boss has gone ballistic.'

Julian tried to hide the fact he'd grown up in a small village in Hampshire by adopting the look and talk of a hood from the Bronx. He wore enough gold to deck out a small jeweller's. Teachers were constantly wincing at the sight of his bottom rising out of his low-slung school uniform.

It was unwise, however, to treat Julian as a joke.

A pair of hands grabbed Winston from behind. His feet left the ground. Pain shot through his body, bringing tears to his eyes. He didn't bother to struggle. He was a thinker, not a man of action.

'We're goin' to the boss's place,' Julian boomed again. 'He's gonna show you. He's gonna teach you respect, geddit?'

Julian tucked Winston under his arm like an American football and strolled down the corridor to Jago's room. Winston struggled to explain that he didn't wish to accompany Julian to Jago's den. But it is hard to explain anything when you are upside down. What would he do with the envelope? If Jago found out Winston had stolen one of his fancy per-sonalised envelopes he'd be toast.

Smee was coming towards them at the head of a bunch of his favourites.

'Let me go, Julian,' Winston yelled loudly, as Smee passed.

Julian grinned at the head. 'Yo. I mean good afternoon, sir. Lovely weather, sir.'

'Having a good time? Fun and games, eh, Tut-Tut.' Smee smiled.

Winston choking in the thug's grip might have been invisible. From his upside-down position, Winston stared at the headmaster's disappearing back and tried to stop himself from hating the man. Smee wasn't worth it. Winston knew that the rot in Duffham, the cowardice and the bullying, started with Smee. The headmaster was a weak man. Picking on those who couldn't fight back made him feel strong. The headmaster had all the power – and Winston had none. Like his mum, who was bossed around all day, Winston had to Do As He Was Told.

But it wouldn't always be that way. He wouldn't

always be around to play the part of Smee's football. One day he'd be doing the kicking.

A few strides later, Julian flung Winston into Jago's room. Winston had gone purple in the face and had difficulty in swallowing. His heart was beating like a rapper's boom box. He was scared.

CHAPTER THREE

Jago's room was pitch black, except for the blinding halogen spotlight trained on Winston. Where had Jago got the spotlight from? Most people didn't have enough fuel to heat their homes and energy-wasting gadgets were banned. Of course, as the son of Sir Giles Lushington, the famous Minister of Defence, Jago didn't play by the normal rules. He used his money and connections to acquire all sorts of privileges. Tucked into the shadows was a console. Winston snorted. It was playing back footage from Jago's CCTV cameras. His second favourite game, after bullying, was spying on the younger kids. He had the first-years' dorms, the common room, the canteen and the staff room covered.

Winston froze. The camera in the common room

had got stuck. It was replaying Winston on a constant loop. How could he have been so careless? He should have checked that he was out of surveillance range.

'You've been a very naughty little boy.' Jago's voice sounded louder in the darkness.

'You bin a naughty boy,' echoed Julian. He was so stupid he always repeated the last thing Jago said.

'You've been trespassing on my patch.'

'You bin trespassing.'

'Shut up, Jules,' Jago snapped.

'Sorry, boss.' Julian lapsed into silence.

'I hear that you've entered the election for school president.' Jago paused. 'I've got news for you, Google. The nearest you'll get to a president is when your mum serves me my school dinners.'

Winston hated people making fun of his mum's job. For a moment his fists bunched, as if he was going to punch Jago.

'You are to remove your name from the list of candidates immediately,' Jago ordered.

'Couldn't we compromise? I could always stand as your deputy,' Winston suggested. His throat felt as if it was stuffed with toilet paper.

'Deputy? I might let you clean my bog if you promised to wash your hands!'

Julian laughed as if Jago had made the funniest joke ever.

'Face it, Google,' Jago continued, 'you're out of your league. Run against me and you'll regret it. You'll be pulling bits of your fingers out of the blender before the week is over.'

'Nice line. But I've heard it before. Was it the man with gold teeth in *Mission: Improbable*?' said Winston. 'Or the bald baddie in *Lethal Payback 5*? I can't quite remember.'

'Quiet, smart arse.' Jago scowled. 'Get out of the race. Or else . . .'

There are times for bravery and times for staying alive. Winston had opened his mouth to admit defeat when –

'Boss?'

'Julian.' Jago was annoyed. 'When are you going to learn to speak when you're spoken to?'

'The cameras.'

Jago whirled around to look at the CCTV. For the fiftieth time, on the video monitor, Winston picked up his pen and wrote on the thick cream envelope. Jago gasped. 'That's mine. That's from my writing case. Daddy's special present. Full body search, Julian. I want that envelope back.'

Julian picked up Winston, pleased with the job he'd been given, and searched his blazer and trouser pockets thoroughly. He even looked in Winston's socks. Finally he had to admit defeat. 'Nah, boss. He's clean, innit?'

Jago scowled. 'Julian, get the headphones.'

'Respect!' Julian's face lit up.

'Do you know what these are?' Jago asked, waving a pair of ordinary-looking headphones.

'Headphones?'

'Headphones. Ha! Do me a favour.' Jago laughed. 'They're aural stereophonoscopes with enhanced magna-plasma neurones. They work by emitting small frequency taser beams that magnify aural sensations by several million gigawatts. The magna-plasma neurones can audify . . . can magnify auditrons and neurones.' He stumbled and came to a stop. 'They'll give you the worst headache in history.'

'I'm sure they're very nasty,' Winston said.

'Nasty? Ha.' Jago scowled. 'Their magna-plasma neuritones . . . er, not neuritrones . . . um . . . neurones, magnify sensory optic – I mean auditory fibres and cause immediate defenestration.'

'Defenestration? I think you'll find defenestration means the act of throwing someone from a window,' Winston pointed out.

For a moment Jago let his confusion show. 'Anyway, *you* couldn't begin to understand these things. They come from the secret naval weapons lab near GCHQ in Cheltenham. They'll make your eardrums go phut!'

'Wow!' Winston took the headphones from Jago and examined the brand name. 'And are they made by Sony?' he asked innocently.

'Idiot, these are the wrong ones,' Jago snapped at Julian, snatching the headphones away from Winston. 'Do I have to do everything myself?' He got up and returned with another pair of headphones, identical except for the manufacturer's name. 'Now these are the magnaplasma stereophonoscopes.' He paused a minute and glared at Winston. 'I'm going to say it in words of one syllable. Give. Me. The. Envelope.'

'Three,' Winston said.

'What?'

'Envelope. It's three syllables.'

'Fine,' said Jago. 'Have it your way.' He nodded to Julian, who fastened the stereophonoscopes on Winston. 'Enjoy,' he said with a cold smile.

Winston sized up the distance to the door. Should he make a run for it? No, Julian would make linguini of him.

'Shall I press play, boss?'

'I'll do the honours.' Jago reached over.

Then God, or the national grid, intervened. The lamps went dead and the room was plunged into darkness. Power cuts were happening all the time these days as the generating companies ran out of fuel. At this rate the world would be going back to horse-drawn carriages and candles any minute now. Winston could hear Jago swearing and Julian crashing into things in the dark.

'Open the curtains, moron,' Jago ordered.

'I'm on the case, boss.'

Winston seized his moment and was halfway out of the door before Julian could even get to the curtains.

As he made his escape, Jago shouted, 'Step out of line, Google, and I'll make you eat your words.'

Winston stopped for a moment and winked. 'I think you'll find I already have,' he said, and was gone.

Running was not Winston's style. But as soon as he was out of Jago's room he strolled briskly till he reached the toilet. He locked the door, then he leaned over the toilet bowl and let it all out. Up came his lunch. He could see broccoli mixed with meatloaf. Nice. Amid the rancid ooze were bits of thick cream paper with navy-blue writing on them. Winston flushed the toilet sadly. How useful that envelope would have been to biographers of the future. Still, as far as he was concerned, it was their loss.

CHAPTER FOUR

The boy was shadow-boxing with a punchbag hanging by a hook from the ceiling. WALLOP. The punchbag shivered in agony. Though the boy was on the wiry side, his strength was frightening. He would have smashed a human to a bloody pulp. Winston watched in awe, his heart in his shoes. For a moment he yearned for Mum, home – even his whingeing sister, Gemma. Were there any sixth-formers in this place who weren't thugs?

Then the boy turned. He had the face of an amiable bloodhound. 'Ah, Wright!' A goofy grin split his face. 'The boy on the telly, heh! Good for you. So you'll be looking after me?'

Winston nodded. He'd dreaded fagging, the Duffham practice where the juniors had to wait on the sixth-formers.

At this very moment Toby Smith was cleaning Julian Tut-Tut's filthy football boots.

'I'm Chaudhury. Hugh Ray-Chaudhury. But call me Hugh! How about making a cuppa? And some buttered toast?'

Winston assumed an expression of innocence.

'You do know how to make tea?'

'Actually, I'm afraid I never learned,' Winston said humbly.

'I see.' Hugo hung up his gloves, towelled the sweat off his face and showed Winston how to make tea. 'You put the tea bag in. Two if you want one.'

'Just milk for me. Thanks.' Winston was always hopeful that his massive milk intake would one day result in a growth spurt.

'Fine. So, tea. Just boil a kettle and add water. Here, I'll show you.'

'I *think* I understand,' Winston said, with little conviction.

'What about toast? How are you on toast?'

'Not very good actually,' Winston admitted, choosing the comfiest chair. 'Could you talk me through toast?'

Winston put his feet up while Hugo bustled around getting the tea together. It wasn't a bad lark, he thought. He could learn to quite like being a fag.

Hugh's study was a far cry from Jago's. An autographed snapshot of the flyweight Prince Naseem hung over the desk. There were cowgirls from *Oklahoma!* and a yodelling Maria from *The Sound of Music*. In pride of place was a magazine snap of Raine Houston, the pretty thirteen-year-old daughter of US President, P.T.O. Houston.

'You into musicals?' Hugh asked, intercepting Winston's glance.

'Um, not really,' Winston admitted.

'I love 'em. I'm hoping to become an actor. But my parents want me to be a doctor. An ear, nose and throat specialist like my uncle Raj.'

A chorus of swirling trumpets that Winston recognised from a musical cut Hugh off. At the same time a loud bleeping came from his digital alarm clock.

'Blast,' Hugh muttered, turning it off and answering the phone at the same time.

'It's the ringtone,' he explained to Winston. '*Cabaret* always sets off my alarm – Oh, hi Mum . . . Yes, yes, yes,' he said into the phone after listening for a while. 'Mum, I've told you I *am* studying . . . all the time . . . We've got chemistry practicals tommorrow. I promise. Yes, I did get the electric toothbrush. Yes, I did gargle. Bye.'

Then, 'My mum,' Hugh explained unnecessarily as he hung up. 'She's crazy about my, um, dental hygiene . . . By the way, did you like my ringtone?'

'Ye-es,' said Winston noncommittally.

'I collect 'em. I've got all the showtunes, crazy polyphonics and monophonics. I've got a fantastic programme that gets you a different ringtone for every caller in your address book. Very useful if you want to avoid your mum.' Hugh stopped and blushed. 'What I mean –'

'I can imagine,' Winston said drily.

'I'll download it for you if you give me your mobile number.'

Though he wasn't particularly interested in ringtones, Winston accepted the offer, touched by Hugh's generosity. And so, between bites of toast, Winston told the older boy about his plans to stand for school president.

Hugh stared at him, puzzled. 'Why?'

'Why not?'

'I mean why do you want to get involved in elections? It's always the smarmy gits who get involved in that stuff. Like Jago. Unless . . .' Hugh brightened as an idea struck him. 'I know. Is it because you want to do good?'

'Do good?' Winston attempted to crush Hugh with a glance. But the sixth-former failed to notice.

'You know, make the world a better place and all that.'

'I think it is naive in the extreme to believe that people are fuelled purely by philanthropic motives. Thinkers from Darwin onwards have demonstrated that self-interest is the key to our survival.'

Hugh blinked. 'Crikey,' he said.

To Winston it was obvious why he wanted to stand for president. But he was finding it hard to put into words – an unusual experience for someone who sounded like he'd swallowed a dictionary.

It had something to do with wanting to be in charge. With not wanting to be bossed around all day long. He didn't believe that people should be content with their lot and follow blindly in their parents' footsteps. Anybody – be they the child of a president or a postman – could do anything. Why should he be a miserable pawn in some hotshot's game? He wanted to make the moves himself.

'I can't just let Jago have it all his own way,' he contented himself with saying.

'Oh, so you want to stand up to Jago?'

'That's it.'

Winston was pushing at an open door with this particular sixth-former.

Hugh was the best featherweight boxer the school had ever had. But underneath his tough exterior beat a heart made of the softest marshmallow. He was the first boy for eighty years to actually refuse to become a prefect, because he thought the system was rotten. Hugh hated to see the younger boys at the mercy of prefects like Jago and Julian, who bullied people just because they could.

By the end of tea, Winston and Hugh were firm friends.

'Same time again tomorrow, Winston?' Hugh put on his boxing gloves as Winston took his leave. 'Many thanks. Excellent toast, that by the way.' Hugh had apparently forgotten that he'd made it.

'Thank you,' said Winston, deadpan. 'So I can rely on your support?'

'Absolutely,' Hugh said as he took a shuddering swing at the punchbag.

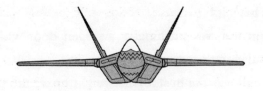

CHAPTER FIVE

'GOVERNMENT HEALTH WARNING – FAGS CAN KILL', the badge read. Underneath in smaller letters ran the line 'VOTE WINSTON'.

Winston pinned it on his sweatshirt and stood back to judge the result in the mirror. He had needed something dramatic to lay before the voters. The answer had hit him like a bolt of rationed electricity. He decided to campaign to abolish fagging. All too often fagging was just an excuse for the Jagos of the world to make life a misery for the Tobys. Plus his campaign would annoy Smee, who revered anything to do with Duffham's traditions.

Winston's 'FAGS CAN KILL' slogan proved a winner and immediately grabbed the school's attention. Gradually more and more kids took to wearing the badges. The prefects couldn't order them to be taken off because freedom of expression was one of the rules of the campaign.

Winston's support among the first-years was soon rock solid. The only boy backing Jago was Jonathan Tut-Tut, who was a mini version his loutish big brother, Julian. But many of the big boys, who'd been fags themselves, didn't see why they shouldn't enjoy the benefits now they were in the upper school.

Winston had another brainwave. Why not campaign to abolish all detentions? Instead boys would have to clean sixth-formers' studies and make their tea as punishment. This went down a storm and it wasn't long before Winston looked set to win the election.

On election day Winston, Jago and their deputies waited backstage with Headmaster Smee. A sweat patch had spread down the back of Jago's shirt. Winston felt quite calm. Or so he told himself. After careful thought, he'd decided to go casual. He was wearing jeans, a Man U sweatshirt and trainers.

He was the first on.

'Nature's law is that the older members of the tribe look after the younger members of the tribe. Duffham's law is that the young waste their best years slaving for the old. It is a travesty of the natural order. Old Mister Darwin would turn in his grave. This isn't the SURVIVAL OF THE FITTEST, it is the SURVIVAL OF THE WEAKEST.'

Winston paused and surveyed the school impressively. He took great care to glance extra long at the TV camera he'd invited along to capture the story for the *Six o'clock news*.

'But I have an even more powerful reason for believing that this slavery should be abolished . . . In the dark days of history, hundreds of thousands of children slaved away in factories and worked in houses making matchboxes and building engines. Those kids grew up half blind and stunted, but the bosses didn't care.' Winston's voice swelled.

'But then a great revolution took place and child labour was abolished. It became illegal to make a child sweat blood for your comfort. It's only in schools such as Duffham that this hideous hangover from the past remains.'

Clapping, cheering and whistling echoed through the hall as Winston came to the end of his speech. 'Go, Winston! Go, Winston!' yelled hundreds of voices.

Winston flew off the stage like a rocket fuelled by

applause. As he passed Jago, the sixth-former glared at him.

'I dunno why you're so pleased with yourself, Google,' he growled. 'In five minutes you'll be history.'

Winston watched Jago stride up to the platform, placed his hands on the lectern and give the audience a big, greasy smile.

'I don't want to bother you all with a long-winded speech. You've heard enough of that to last you a lifetime. My pitch to you is short, sweet and practical. I'm sure you've all heard of my dad, Sir Giles Lushington.' He pointed to the man in the front row.

Sir Giles was about fifty. With his bald head and glittering eyes, he looked like a python in a pinstripe suit.

'Daddy has kindly agreed to stump up some funding. If I become Duffham's president, every single one of you will get a Himouchi Compact 22000 EX Pro games console. Plus a bumper hamper of chocs and sweets.' Jago broke into a smile which he probably thought was charming. 'I even include my opponent, Winston Wright, in this offer.'

On cue, Julian shuffled on stage, carrying a Harrods hamper in one hand and the games console in the other. 865 schoolboys drew in their breaths as one. The prototype 22000 EX Pro games console. It's sheeny surface itching for their index fingers. Chocolates oozing out of the hamper. Winston could almost touch their greed.

The whole election was a stitch-up! Lushington was going straight for the voters' pockets.

Winston felt a calming hand on his shoulder. 'Don't worry,' said Hugh. 'People aren't gonna be bought by Sir Giles's dosh. No one can stand Jago.'

Winston tensed. He knew people said one thing in public, but when it came to it they would vote with their bellies.

As he watched people cast their votes, he caught sight of his mum behind the Minister of Defence. Winston tried to suppress a wave of unworthy embarrassment. Compared with Sir Giles, his mum and Gemma looked like Ford Fiestas at a Ferrari conference. Where did they get their clothes?

Finally the hour was up.

Headmaster Smee led Winston and Jago out on stage, along with their deputies Ray-Chaudhury and Tut-Tut. Smee surveyed the audience, smiling bland-ly. 'It's been a vewy intewesting campaign. Lots of thwills and spills. What I say is let the best man win.'

Smee made a big charade of opening the envelope and miming surprise.

But Winston *knew* he'd lost as soon as the headmaster glanced down at the result. Smee couldn't stop his delight showing.

'Well, well. Vewy, vewy intewesting. It's been close. Vewy close, vewy close indeed,' Smee blathered. 'The result is Winston Wight 425 votes, Jago Lushington 440 votes. I therefore have gweat pleasure in declawing Jago Lushington this year's pwesident.'

Jago ran up to the headmaster and shook his hand, punching the air in triumph. Through a red mist, Winston saw Smee pinning the president's badge on his blazer. Sir Giles was in on the act, striding on stage to congratulate his son. Winston knew his mum would never have dared come on stage if he had won.

Jago had decided to play at being gracious in his acceptance speech. 'A great day for me and for Duffham Hall.' He beamed. 'While five per cent of me is sad for my opponent, Winston Wright, who ran a pretty slick campaign, the other fifty per cent is just thrilled to be your new president.'

A gale of laughter swallowed the rest of Jago's speech. Maths had never been his forte. Sir Giles looked peeved.

But Winston scarcely noticed Jago's gaffe. War drums were beating in his ears. How he did it he didn't know. It was a miracle . . .

As the laughter subsided, somehow he found himself walking up to his hated opponent and congratulating him. He offered to 'work in partnership with Jago Lushington and his dad, the honourable Minster of Defence, whom I have always considered one of the few visionary politicians we have left in this country. I am willing to serve as Jago's deputy,' he found himself saying, as if in a dream. 'I want Duffham to be an example of fairness that inspires schools across the country.'

The hall resounded with applause. Those who'd voted for Julian salved their guilty consciences by clapping the hardest.

Sir Giles walked up to Winston and shook his hand. 'Well done, my boy,' he said, 'very statesmanlike.'

Cheers and yells of, 'Winston, Winston, Winston,' swept across the hall.

Perhaps, Winston thought, failure could sometimes be more *interesting* than success.

Jago tried to butt in between Winston and his dad. 'Don't talk to that kid, Daddy,' he hissed. 'He's a freak from another planet.'

'Nonsense. His speech was terrific. You'd do well to study it,' Sir Giles replied sharply.

After the vote, tea and biscuits were served in the assembly hall. Gemma had disappeared, probably off with some of the sixth-formers. Mum stood in the crush, making polite conversation with Headmaster Smee. More accurately, Smee made polite conversation while Mum stood there looking dazed and very shy.

She perked up when Winston came over. 'Well done,' she said, giving him a warm hug. She had taken off her jacket and was wearing a pink Crimplene blouse.

Winston wished, again, he could spend some money on her. Once, when he had given her a top-of-the-range mobile, she had been unable to figure out how to use it. A couple of weeks later he saw it in the window of the church charity shop where she bought her clothes.

'I'm so proud of you, Winnie,' Mum said.

Winston stiffened. 'Shhh, Mum, not that name. Anyway, didn't you notice I lost?'

'Course you did,' said Mum. 'But you lost in style.'

Winston was surprised to feel a surge of emotion. For a moment he couldn't say anything at all.

Later Winston found Toby at work with a scrubbing

brush. The whole wall of the common room had been covered in graffiti. 'Toby.' The redhead turned round. Winston noticed that his jacket was torn and his eye was beginning to puff up. 'What happened?'

'It was Jago,' Toby said, biting back a sob. 'He ripped off my badge. Said I wouldn't be needing it any more. Then, when my blazer was all ruined, he got Tut-Tut to give me a slap round the face for having a torn blazer.'

'Patience,' Winston said quietly.

'He said I wasn't wearing the regulation school uniform. He's going to report me.'

'I'll take care of it.'

'But . . . I hate them.'

'I'm not over-fond of them myself.'

'I want to run away. Duffham stinks.'

Winston sighed, then he looked Toby squarely in the eyes. 'You know what they say about revenge, don't you, Toby?'

'What?'

'It's a dish best eaten cold.'

PARADISE LOST

Scratch, scratch, scratch went something in the darkness. The noise woke Lucy up. She shivered and pulled her blanket up to her chin. Was there a rat poking about in the cellar? Or worse, a snake?

The old Lucy Carter – the girl who loved sleepovers and peanut butter and jam sandwiches – would have run screaming to her dad at the mere rustle of a rat.

But that girl was dead. The new Lucy wasn't freaked by a rat. A rodent isn't really something to be scared of. Not when you've seen your father kidnapped and swallowed by a submarine and the rest of your family have disappeared. She rolled over in her bed of hay and checked the time on her illuminated watch: 9 a.m. She hoped someone would come today. No one had been for two days and Lucy was getting hungry. She could do without a full belly. But being thirsty was unbearable. Her throat ached. What if no one came? If the thugs had got them too? What would happen to her? Would she starve? No. She would survive somehow. Whatever happened, she wouldn't let her father down.

Lucy flicked on her torch and shone it around the dark corners of the cellar. Nothing except the bits of old combine harvester that were stored here.

Then she saw the rat. It was sitting right in the centre of the floor, nibbling at something it held in its paws. It took a look at Lucy with its bright eyes, then scampered away up the ladder to the outside world. Lucy was jealous of the rat. For a moment she considered climbing up the ladder, out of the trapdoor and to the freedom and sunshine of a summer morning. Except it wasn't really freedom. Not when the men were looking for her.

There weren't many things that frightened Lucy any more. But she was scared of the thug with diamonds in his teeth spelling L-O-V-E and H-A-T-E, the man who smelt of death.

Feet sounded on the wooden floor overhead. Heavy feet, too big for a rat. Lucy tensed, waiting. These were not footsteps she knew.

CHAPTER SIX

'You know what I think of you, Google, you freak from the planet Zog,' Jago began pleasantly. He was sprawled on his double bed at the Lushingtons' London mansion. His pet poodle, Fang, bared its teeth at Winston, ready to bite.

'You've made it quite clear, Jago,' Winston replied courteously.

'Shut up. I don't think your sort are fit to lick Daddy's boots, let alone work in his office. Who are you? A nobody. I'll have you know Sir Giles is the sixteenth Baron Lushington. Our family lived in castles while your family were swinging through the trees.'

'I don't think my ancestors ever went in for gymnastics. They were probably at home counting the coconuts.'

'Don't get lippy with me. I've had it up to here with your cheek.'

It was three months after Winston had lost the school election. His reward for impressing the minister was a holiday job at the Ministry of Defence – in Sir Giles Lushington's private office. He was staying with the minister's family at their grand mansion near the House of Commons.

Winston's mum had begged him to come with her to Bournemouth for their summer holiday. He'd a weakness for candyfloss and roller-coaster rides. He could even have put up with Gemma's whingeing. And his mum was certainly better company than the starchy Lushingtons.

But the opportunity to get inside government was too good to miss. The problem was Jago. He was eaten up with jealousy.

When Daddy had got his son work experience, Jago had rigged up a CCTV surveillance system of the staff. A computer buff had discovered the system after a routine sweep for bugs. At first there'd been suspicion that Arab oil interests had been to blame. But soon the finger pointed firmly at Jago.

Outraged secretaries had threatened to quit. Penpushers had consulted their lawyers. His pampered only son had fallen several notches in Sir Giles's estimation. Jago's work experience ended abruptly.

So Jago had not taken the news of Winston's holiday job well. On his second day with the Lushingtons, Jago had invited Winston up to his room for a chat. Winston came prepared for trouble.

'I'll be watching you. Put a step wrong and I'll get some of my little electronic friends to see to you. Remember the stereophonoscopes?'

'How could I forget? Their effect on Julian was, er . . . sad.'

Jago went deep red. 'Yeah, well. That was an accident. Anyway, as I say, I've got nastier things here.' He held up a set of wires with an ordinary plug socket and some nodes at the end. 'You know what these are?'

'Not headphones, I trust.'

'WILL YOU, SHUDDUP?'

'You did ask,' Winston said reasonably.

'These babies will give you such bad electric shocks you'll beg for mercy. The gadget came in useful in certain Latin American countries my dad does business with. If you do anything wrong . . .'

'I try not to do things that are morally wrong. Can I go now please?'

'Morality? What's that got to do with anything?' Jago looked puzzled. 'Now get lost.'

Winston walked slowly out of Jago's room, his face a study in inscrutability.

Sir Giles was sitting at a vast ebony desk in his office. He had a pile of documents and an open red box in front of him.

'Sorry to intrude, Sir. It's an urgent matter.'

'Spit it out.'

'I've enjoyed my stay here, Sir Giles. But I'm afraid I'm going to have to say goodbye.'

'What?' Sir Giles frowned.

'I've been threatened. Perhaps you would lend an ear to this?'

Winston took a bog-standard mini cassette recorder out of his pocket and pressed play. He believed you didn't need high-tech spy hardware to defeat an enemy. All you needed was brains.

Sir Giles looked as if he was sucking on a lemon as he listened to his son squeaking out of the tape recorder. 'The stupid idiot,' he blurted when Jago started boasting about his contacts in Latin America. Sir Giles lunged for the off switch. 'This stuff could do me serious political damage if it got into the wrong hands. I mean after the last time. My God, I'd be finished.' Sir Giles recollected himself. 'Pure fantasy on Jago's part, you understand.'

'Of course, Sir Giles.'

'Winston, you've done very well. Very well indeed. You've exposed a big flaw in my domestic security operation. I'm going to see to it that all my son's little pieces of equipment are confiscated. He's shown he can't be trusted. After I've finished with him he won't dare to come near you again, never mind threaten you.'

Winston turned to go, his plan complete. Jago wouldn't be able to bully him any more!

Then the minister called him back. 'My boy,' he said, his voice uncharacteristically uncertain. 'Would you like to come to parliament with me today? For prime minister's Questions. You know, the bit where the opposition gets to grill the PM?'

'Of course I know. I'd be delighted.'

'Generally only MPs can sit on the benches in the House. But the Speaker, the man in charge, you know, owes me a favour. I think he'll make an exception for you. After all, you are an exceptional case.'

Winston smiled modestly. He'd found that the best way to deal with flattery was, well, to just accept it. But underneath he was totally thrilled.

At last! This was more like it! Jago was neutralised. And Winston was leaving schoolboy games behind.

CHAPTER SEVEN

Winston's appearance at Sir Giles Lushington's side on the government front bench caused a bit of stir. It was the first time in anyone's memory that a child had appeared in the House. He was three decades younger than most MPs, not to mention a good deal shorter.

'Who's the kid?' the journalists in the press gallery wondered. Was he some kind of mascot?

Some thought it was the minister's son, others that he was something to do with a new Children's Bill.

Winston sat on the green-baize benches and drank it all in: the hundreds of suited MPs, the TV cameras, the gilded roof and plush carpet. The place stank of power. Winston felt strangely at home. It was like being back at school, only on a scale that really let him breathe. The prime minister was the headmaster. The

Cabinet ministers were the prefects. And the back-benchers, the humble lobby-fodder MPs, were the rank-and-file schoolboys.

John Minor was droning on about energy. Though the Prime Minister was the most powerful man in the country he had all the charisma of a burst water main. When he talked the country tended to go to sleep.

Then Dame Stella Curry, the Leader of the Opposition party, stood up to ask an question. 'Could the Prime Minister tell the House about the mysterious Sheikh Ali al-Yamani? This man is forming his own army. He bought his first oil company in Saudi Arabia six months ago and is now bidding for BritOil. What is the government doing to stop him?' Dame Curry added with an unpleasant smile, 'And could the PM also let us know, are children running the country now? I would have invited my grandson along if someone had told me.'

The house exploded with laughter. The Prime Minister stood up. He was jingling change in his jacket pocket. Ill at ease, Winston realised.

Suddenly the house was plunged into darkness. Another power cut. Winston saw the TV camera opposite him flicker and grow black. There was a chorus of groans and hoots from fed-up MPs. A second later the lights came back on.

'Maybe children should take over the government,' a wit on the back benches called out. 'They'd probably do it better than John Minor.'

The Prime Minister ignored the interruption. He was listening to Sir Giles, who was whispering something in his ear.

'The Defence Minister informs me that his guest is a remarkable young man, Winston Wright. You may recall that Winston has featured on the news,' the PM declared. 'As far as the mysterious Ali al-Yamani goes, the government is keeping contact with him to a minimum. Um, we are very concerned with his activities and are keeping an eye on him. That is all I have to say on the matter, um, at the moment.' The PM's monotonous voice could make even a global threat sleep-inducing.

Winston, however, was wide awake. Call it gut instinct, but he felt there was something not quite right about the Saudi Arabian sheikh. In fact, only yesterday he had dispatched Hugh to Companies House to investigate. Quickly he scribbled on a piece of paper and handed it to Sir Giles. Sir Giles looked at the note, raised his eyebrows and handed it on to the PM, who was stumbling along.

'I've a note from our schoolboy friend here,' the PM continued with renewed vigour. 'It says that, contrary to popular belief, Ali al-Yamani bought his first oil company in Uzbekistan eighteen months ago. Winston has proof. Things have come to a pretty pass when a child knows more than you lot of duffers.'

MPs roared with laughter. Soon after, amid more jeering, the House broke for tea. As Winston and Sir Giles left, a few MPs ruffled Winston's hair and slapped him on the back to congratulate him on his research. Winston took the back-slapping well, trying his best not to show his irritation. He wasn't comfortable with people treating him like a pet puppy.

'Hello, my little man.' Dame Curry prodded him in the ribs with a finger the size of a sausage. 'What are you doing here?'

'I'm on work experience,' Winston replied curtly, stiffening and moving out of range of her forceful fingers.

'With him?' Dame Curry nodded towards Sir Giles. 'You better be careful, son. You know we call him the "Prince of Darkness".'

'I'm quite aware of Sir Giles's sobriquet and I consider it a compliment,' Winston said coolly. 'I believe your nickname, Dame Curry, is "Tankgirl".'

Dame Curry gasped, taken aback.

Sir Giles laughed. 'I think you'll find my protégé punches above his weight, Stella. Come along now, Winston.'

Winston made to follow Sir Giles but bumped straight into the Prime Minister. His heart raced. He had bumped into *the PM*.

John Minor smiled. 'You should think of going into politics, Winston. You'd make an impressive Member of Parliament in twenty years or so.'

'I'm not sure I can wait that long, PM.'

Minor blinked through his thick spectacles. 'You're a young man in a hurry, I see.'

'Yes.'

There was something disconcerting about Winston's direct stare, something that could make even a PM feel a bit muddled.

'Prime Minister,' Sir Giles said, laying his hand on Minor's arm. 'I wonder if you might consider taking Winston into your private office for a few days. He's exceptionally well informed about energy issues, you know. Could be useful.'

'Why not? Drop by tomorrow,' the PM said vaguely as he was quickly shepherded away by his minder, before he could agree to any more favours.

Winston kept up with Sir Giles as he swept along to his suite of offices. They were some of the most impressive in Parliament, featuring deep leather armchairs and ceilings covered with golden angels. Sir Giles beckoned him into his private office. 'Good stuff, Winston. Impressive background research.'

Winston smiled. It was one of the things he most appreciated about Sir Giles. There was no rib tickling with him. He didn't treat him like a half-wit just because he was twelve years old.

The minister had many detractors. Eight years ago, Sir Giles had been snapped by a photographer at the Alka Salsa nightclub. He was standing on the bar wearing lipstick, a feathered headdress and a grass hula-hula skirt.

His drunken Indian squaw impersonation turned him into a national joke. His powerful friends deserted him. He looked finished. But somehow he'd managed to claw his way up the greasy pole again. The new Sir Giles was a changed man who hadn't touched alcohol since that fateful night.

'You are clearly up to speed with al-Yamani. This is his MI5 file.' Sir Giles gave Winston a wad of papers in a maroon folder marked 'TOP SECRET'.

'Discretion is vital. Don't speak of the contents of this file to anyone.' In his agitation Sir Giles began to pace the room. 'I have put you into the PM's office for a special reason, Winston. You are young. You can get to places no adult would be able to. You are also exceptionally . . . er . . . switched on. Keep your eyes and ears open while you are around the Prime Minister. I've heard some frightening rumours. If you hear anything of al-Yamani tell me immediately. And remember, don't use the telephone. Come straight to me.'

'I'll be careful, sir.'

'You can't be *too* careful. This is dangerous. We don't really know who we're up against.'

CHAPTER EIGHT

'If I don't look after you who will?'

The silky voice came from behind the closed door of the Prime Minister's office. It was more of a murmur than a voice, suggesting someone so discreet he could disappear in a puff of wind.

'I don't need anyone to look after me. I *am* the Prime Minister.'

'Of course you are,' the voice soothed. 'Remember what I've said. Keep a look-out all the time.'

'All right,' came the PM's grumpy reply.

'Who's that with the PM?' Winston asked Minor's secretary, a sensible middle-aged woman.

'I can't tell you that. We're not allowed to know.'

The door opened and out came a man in beige. He scanned Winston in a flash. The boy had the impression he was being committed to memory.

'Ah, so you're the famous Winston,' the man said. 'I've heard about you. Perhaps when you've finished here you'd care to pay me a visit? Room 1010.'

'Certainly,' Winston said politely. 'Who should I ask for?'

'Just remember Room 1010.'

Before Winston could get a grip on him, the man had disappeared. When Winston tried to remember what he looked like, he couldn't. Was he a spy?

The secretary ushered Winston into the PM's office. He savoured the moment as his feet sank into thick purple carpet. So this was it! The pulsing heart of power in England. The place where all the really big decisions were taken.

Actually, it was a bit of a let-down.

Winston didn't know what he'd imagined, but not this: a battered desk and mouldy old armchairs. The walls were dotted with pictures of Minor's two blonde daughters. Something about the girls reminded Winston of the Queen's corgis. The dogs, the PM and the daughters all had the same sad eyes and snub noses.

John Minor himself was sitting in a rocking chair, his feet on a small coffee table, red box open in front of him. There were dozens of papers in it, some with technical drawings of windmills and solar power plants. He looked bored. 'I'll see to the young man,' he said to his secretary.

'Thank you, Prime Minister.' She closed the door softly.

'Nice lady. Has a bit of a tendency to report to GQ.'

'Who's GQ?'

'Who? Nobody at all. Now, Winston, tell me about yourself. What are you keen on?'

'Mainly foreign affairs. Particularly the Middle East and the Far East. I follow the energy markets. I keep a close eye on developments in the alternative-energy sector. It really is important for Britain to think about the future.'

John Minor looked blank. 'Tell you what. How about a cuppa? How are you on tea?'

Winston was conscious of a curious feeling that he'd lived through this scene before. Recently.

'Energy policy, eh?' John Minor said, busy with the tea things.

Winston nodded. 'It's a fascinating area. I believe there is a year, max, of oil reserves in the Middle East and former Soviet Union. Of course, there is interesting research going on at Cambridge, but the crunch might come sooner than we think. We have to be prepared for the day when the oil runs out. I'd like to be involved in the disaster planning. We need to be bold.'

'Quite so, quite so,' John Minor said vaguely. He stuck his hands in his pockets and took out a packet of Walkers cheese and onion crisps. He began to munch them thoughtfully.

Winston waited.

'Do you like games?' the Prime Minister asked at last.

'I think role-playing is certainly an interesting option. It might help us to envisage the task faced by the emergency services – how to care for the elderly, get people to work and so on.'

John Minor didn't seem to have heard. 'I like Scrabble best. I got five seven-letter words yesterday, including AQUATIC. The Q was on the triple word score. I like Risk and Monopoly and I'm quite good on the old PlayStation. But I like board games best. Did you know, I'm the Westminster Monopoly champ?'

'Er . . . we could try a game of Scrabble,' Winston said hesitantly.

'Goody. Scrabble!' The PM jumped up excitedly and fetched the board. 'We might just be able to fit in a quick game before I'm due at committee. Wind farms, I think it is.'

'I confess I'd be more interested in your ideas on wind farms. I, er –'

John Minor cut him off. 'No. No! NO! Boring.' He began setting out the Scrabble board. 'I must warn you that no one in this building has been able to beat me at Scrabble. I'm pretty good, even if I say so myself.'

The PM wasn't boasting. He was indeed good at Scrabble, though he did have the annoying habit of taking ages over his turn. Winston, however, was *brilliant* at the game. He could instantly spot letter combinations and anagrams. His mind processed the possibilities in a flash.

After Winston got three seven-letter words in a row the PM began to get edgy. It was definitely time for tact. Winston put CART down on the board instead of Czarist and the PM unconsciously let out a sigh of relief. The game proceeded more smoothly after that, with Winston contributing such beauties as TENT and MAN.

Then there was a knock on the door. The PM had taken his phone off the hook so they wouldn't be disturbed. 'Come,' he said grumpily, and his secretary stuck her head through the door.

She looked disapproving when she saw the Scrabble board. 'You're wanted in the briefing room, sir. It's URGENT.'

'I never get a moment's peace in this place,' the PM grumbled. 'You wait here, Winston, and no cheating, mind! I'd better take the bag of letters. Keep temptation away.'

With that the PM was gone, leaving Winston alone in the office.

For a few seconds Winston sat quite still in his chair, making sure the PM wasn't coming back. He scanned the room, taking in the large picture over the mantelpiece of a village with a pretty pond. Road's End, Shropshire, said the brass plaque underneath. Then he drew on a pair of thin nylon gloves and started with the papers on the desk, making sure he left everything exactly as it was afterwards. All the while he kept an ear open for the PM's return. He went through the red box full of energy papers and flicked through the filing cabinet. Nothing suspicious there.

His mind went back to the contents of the al-Yamani file as he worked. The Arab was a sinister operator who moved in the shadows. MI5, the CIA and the Russians had put their best spies on his case

– but there were still only blurry photos of the man and little solid evidence of what he was up to. But there were disturbing rumours. He was acquiring dangerous weaponry: decommissioned submarines, intercontinental warheads, even nuclear material.

By the window, next to an overflowing waste-paper basket, was a document shredder – a white Xerox machine. Winston looked through the basket, but it didn't contain anything very interesting: just more crisp packets and some half-eaten Starbursts.

Then Winston went for Minor's computer. Quickly he opened the email account. The machine asked him for a password. He tried the names of Minor's wife and daughters. No luck.

Then, with a sudden burst of hope, Road's End, the name of the Shropshire village. He had struck lucky. Minor's account opened up to Winston. There were hundreds of emails, but the one from 'Ali' had to be the most interesting. Winston scanned it, then quickly printed it out, closing the email as he did so.

Winston heard the door opening. Minor was back. Hastily, he stuffed the printout into his trouser pocket.

'No cheating while I was away?' Minor strode in. Seeing Winston's flushed appearance, his eye travelled suspiciously to the large *Oxford English Dictionary* behind his desk. If he noticed Winston's gloves he didn't comment. 'Haven't been looking up seven-letter words, I hope?'

'Cheating's not my style,' Winston said smoothly. His hand touched the crumpled paper in his pocket.

'I could never stand a cheat, young Winston,' the PM boomed, sitting down. He was still clutching the bag of Scrabble letters. 'I say. Young Winston. Has anyone ever called you that before? Reminds me of your namesake, Winston Churchill. Led the country through World War Two, as you know. I met him once actually.'

'Really?'

'He came to my estate in Dulwich. Opening a new bridge he was. I shook his hand. I was only about eight but he made a big impression on me. Huge man. Huge personality.' John Minor smiled at Winston. 'You should adopt him as your role model.'

Winston came close to blushing. 'I think all I have in common with Churchill is arrogance.'

'Arrogance? Not a bad quality for a politician. Always been a bit arrogant myself. No one could ever beat me at Scrabble, even as a kid. And my Monopoly game speaks for itself.'

But Winston wasn't listening. He had liked Minor.

The PM wasn't what you'd call brainy, but he gave off a strong smell of decency. He was the kind of man you'd want as an uncle; one who would never forget to give you a couple of crisp banknotes when he visited.

But if he was reading the email right, the Prime Minister's likeable-guy image was an elaborate deception. The man was as rotten as they come.

CHAPTER NINE

Winston trickled into the office silently. Sir Giles was typing on his computer. For a few moments Winston watched the reflection of the computer screen in the mirror behind the minister's desk. Then he coughed.

Sir Giles stopped typing and flushed scarlet.

'I'm afraid that I have some alarming news, Sir Giles. Regarding the PM.' Winston didn't believe in wasting time on pleasantries. Especially when what he had to say was far from pleasant.

'And Ali al-Yamani?'

'How did you know?'

'I've had my suspicions for some time. What've you found?'

Winston put the email on the minister's desk.

Same time. Hampton Village Hotel. The Anne Boleyn Suite. No security please. Thanks for your help organising this caper. Your reward, big bucks up for grabs! Regards, Ali.

Sir Giles read the note slowly. Then read it again. 'I'm hardly surprised,' he said at last. 'Another rotten apple in the political barrel . . .'

'Not surprised? I'm astounded. I never read him as a crook. Why did you think Minor might be on the take?'

'Never mind that now.'

'I *need* to know.'

'Al-Yamani came up in Cabinet discussions. There was some talk of changing the law. Making it illegal for foreign nationals to buy shares in BritOil. The PM was against the idea. So was the energy minister. They vetoed the proposal. I thought their actions were suspicious. Anti-British.' Sir Giles got up and walked restlessly over to the painting of his knightly ancestor hanging over the fireplace. He stood looking at it, his back to Winston.

Winston had noticed that the minister seemed to draw strength from the painting of the tenth Baron

Lushington. The nature of the encouragement he received couldn't have been artistic. Winston had seen more attractive cheeseburgers.

'What are you going to do about this?' Sir Giles turned round and faced him.

'Me? Do?'

'Yes, yes. Our national interests are at stake.'

'Have you got any ideas, sir?'

Sir Giles blanched. 'I can't get mixed up in this. Too big for me.'

'Too big for *you*.'

Sir Giles looked embarrassed. 'We've never talked about it, Winston, but I've had my troubles in the past. You've heard the gossip?'

Winston nodded, remembering the talk about Sir Giles's problems with alcohol.

'It was mere youthful foolishness. However, I paid a heavy price. I became a laughing stock.'

'But you survived, sir.'

'Yes, I survived.' Sir Giles's sad smile suggested he'd suffered in the process. 'But I can't take getting mixed up in another political scandal. *You* found the note. I'm afraid you're on your own.'

'What about MI5. Put a tail on the PM?'

Sir Giles shook his head. 'We don't know how

deep this thing goes. We can't trust anyone.'

'I'm not exactly the trusting type,' Winston replied.

'There is only one possible course of action. You've got to take the email to the press. To the *Stun*, for example.'

'The *Stun*? They hardly have a reputation for being truthful. Or careful with the facts.'

'If you don't like the *Stun*, how about the *Sunday Scandal*? They'd love it. Any paper would. They have the resources for investigative work.'

'I'll think about it, Sir Giles. Very carefully.' Winston got up, returning the email to his pocket. 'I have to get back to the PM's office.'

Sir Giles gave Winston a searching look. 'Take care, Winston. That email is dynamite.' He paused, the words drumming in Winston's head. 'Always let me know where you are.'

'I'll do my best.'

Winston made to leave, but something bothered him about the way he had found the email. It was too neat, too pat. Had someone sent Minor a deliberately vague and suspicious-sounding email to frame him? But how could they know that the email would be found? Winston couldn't condemn the PM without knowing all the facts. He had to delve to the bottom of this dirty pond himself. He would have to trail John Minor, even if it was dangerous.

Sir Giles seemed to read his mind. 'Don't even think of trying to go it alone on this one. Some people would kill for that email.'

'Surely *murder* is taking things a bit far,' Winston said with a grin.

Sir Giles didn't return the smile 'This is no joking matter. I don't want to be the one ringing up the undertakers to order your coffin.'

CHAPTER TEN

A dark figure was waiting for Winston under an orange street lamp.

Hugh looked vaguely threatening in his black leather jacket, leather trousers and studded boots. No wonder people returning home after an evening out crossed the street to avoid him. Smoke curled from his cupped palm and drifted up into the night. A disapproving frown crossed Winston's face as he looked at his friend.

'Cigarettes? Odd choice of vice for a boxer.'

'It's not a cigarette. It's a cigar. I enjoy them after a good dinner. Besides, I need to calm my nerves tonight.'

'I'm not a killjoy, but smoking is out of date, Hugh. I won't bore you with the statistics. But if you enjoy playing games with your life, try Russian roulette. Probably safer.'

'It's just a cigar.'

Winston unflipped his Blackberry, a mobile phone-cum-pocket computer-cum-video camera. He had bought it after the incident with Jago, realising he had to upgrade his personal technology. He opened it and showed Hugh the way to the Hampton Village Hotel on the mini LCD screen.

'Why we doing this?' Hugh demanded. 'It could be dangerous. Why don't we take the email to the *Stun*, like Sir Giles suggested? I don't see that we gain –'

Winston ignored him. 'I take it you've got the car?' he said, returning the Blackberry to the pocket of his parka.

Hugh looked embarrassed. 'Actually, er, yes. But it's not quite – Look, I couldn't get any petrol – our ration card is empty. But that thing runs on diesel, which I managed to get hold of.'

Winston looked at the rusting Peugeot by the kerb and sighed. 'Don't worry. I might be meeting some-one who can help. But I don't know if he'll turn up.'

'Ahem.' A cough sounded in the darkness behind them. A nondescript man had suddenly materialised. He was wearing a trench coat and a trilby hat. 'Hello, Winston,' the man said.

Winston held out his hand. 'Hello, GQ.'

The man bowed his head politely. 'I think you'll find this will do,' he said.

A monster of a black and red motorbike was parked near Smita's Convenience Store. Huge Harley emblems gleamed on its massive fenders. The thing was the size of a small car.

'It's a Lava Red Sun Glow,' gasped Hugh.

'*What?*' said Winston.

'A Harley-Davidson Road King classic, complete with a twin-cam 88 isolation-mounted engine. It's a fuel-injected heat-managed marvel of modern engineering design. I'd *love* to have one but they cost about £14,000.'

'It's a nice little bike,' GQ agreed.

'It handles like a red-hot breeze. You could blaze across the Gobi desert or glide up Mount Everest in that thing,' Hugh enthused.

The boxer was almost swooning.

'Control yourself, Hugh. If you were any more breathless you'd be dead.' Winston took in the long black leather seat. He supposed he could fit comfortably behind Hugh on it.

'There are one or two, um, modifications to the bike,' GQ murmured. 'I think you'll find them useful. If there's nothing else I'll be off.'

Winston turned round to thank him, but the spy had already vanished.

'It's *cool*,' Winston said, fastening on the helmet. 'But it won't be cool if people are shooting at us, will it? Nothing to stop the bullets.'

Hugh's grin faltered. 'Crikey. Do you think that's likely?'

Winston shrugged. 'I wonder if GQ planned it that way. Anyway, it's too late to worry. Come on, we'll be late.'

Hugh hopped on the bike and Winston swung up behind. With a deep throb of power, the motorbike started up and the boys were off. Adrenaline flooded Winston's veins. The roaring motorbike possessed a heart of its own.

There was hardly any traffic. People rarely drove out in the evenings for pleasure, as petrol was too scarce to waste. Before long they were flashing through the shadowy trees of Green Park. On the approach to the King's Road they were nearly hit by a supermarket lorry, which swerved just at the last minute.

'Maniacs,' the driver yelled, shaking his fist.

Winston's heart missed several beats.

'Hugh,' he shouted when he had regained his power of speech, 'you *have* passed your test?'

'What?' Hugh bellowed above the noise of wind and traffic.

'Your driving test, you *have* passed?'

'What?'

'Slow down,' Winston yelled.

Hugh did so and Winston repeated the question.

'Course I did. You know that. Fourth attempt.'

'Not that test. Your motorbike test. You've got to pass it to take a passenger.'

'Have you?'

With a twist of the accelerator, Hugh was off again, swerving within inches of a maroon camper van. Soon they crossed the river and were in south London. The grand mansions gave way to houses crammed together like packets of cornflakes on a conveyer belt. Then on to the leafy suburbs, where the houses thinned out and fields and trees took their place.

'Odd place for a luxury hotel,' Winston shouted.

'What?' Hugh turned his head.

'Never mind,' Winston yelled, fearful of a crash.

Finally Hampton Village Hotel came into view. They parked the bike. Moving in the shadows of a derelict tower block, they surveyed the hotel. It was designed to look like a Tudor castle, complete with turrets and ramparts. It was surrounded by a moat and a drawbridge. There were security guards dressed as sixteenth-century soldiers in red breeches and tights by the front door. The windows were barred. There were no drainpipes. The Hampton Village Hotel was as solid as a fortress.

'This really is taking the Tudor theme too far,' Winston whispered. Then he pointed to a figure about 100 yards away. Standing by a black Jaguar was the PM's trusted driver.

'Minor must be inside the hotel,' Hugh whispered.

Winston nodded.

'Do you want me to see if I can take out some of the security guards? We might be able to make a run for it. There are only about ten of them.'

'Don't get carried away,' Winston warned. 'We're a couple of schoolkids, not an SAS hit squad. Have you seen the size of those security guys? We've got to use our brains.'

Two waiters dressed as beefeaters were coming out of the kitchen doors. One was long and stringy, the other a short, plump woman.

'Wait a moment.' A gleam had come into Hugh's eyes. 'Don't go away.'

Before Winston had time to reply, Hugh was heading towards the kitchen. Moments later Winston's heart sank as he saw a large shadow rearing on the white walls outside the kitchen. He heard the noise of scuffles and shouts.

Hugh then reappeared, holding something in his hands.

'You coming or what?' he called.

CHAPTER ELEVEN

'Little rats,' the hotel security guard muttered as he stripped the beefeater costumes off the wriggling Winston and Hugh. 'Bleeding kids. Playing stupid games. You're lucky I'm not calling the police.' Instead the guard opened the window of the second-floor hotel suite. He took the boys by the scruff of the neck and dropped them out of the window. First Winston, then Hugh.

They landed with a soft thud in a flower bed full of roses.

'Ouch,' Hugh cried as a thorn pierced his bottom.

'Don't you go spoiling our roses,' the guard yelled, and closed the window with a bang.

'Well, that was a great plan,' Winston hissed sarcastically. 'Our clothes are torn and we look like we've been mud-wrestling.'

'It always works in the movies. I'm sure I've seen Spiderman or someone do –'

'There's a big difference between Spiderman and Hugh Ray-Chaudhury. He's a fictional character, you're a schoolboy.'

Hugh reddened.

'Anyway,' Winston continued. 'We didn't have the door code, did we? Room service waiters need a code to get around a hotel.'

'I didn't know,' Hugh said defensively. 'I didn't think –'

'Precisely! You didn't know. Or think. Never again am I going to dress up as a fat midget in a skirt.'

Hugh grinned at the memory. 'You looked great. Made a lovely girl.'

'We can't stay in the mud.' Winston scowled. 'Come on.'

A shamefaced Hugh and a grumpy Winston trudged across the car park. They made for the tumbledown tower block where they'd parked the bike. Most of the windows in the building were broken, and the walls were covered with graffiti. It was an odd eyesore. It looked more like something you'd get in a run-down inner city than opposite a glittering five-star hotel.

Winston glanced up at the skyscraper. On the tenth floor a weak light was flickering in one of the windows. 'Lets go up there.'

'Why?'

'I want to find out why a light's burning.'

'If you say so. It's probably just a tramp.'

The boys pushed through the front door and climbed up a filthy stairwell. It was covered with broken glass and plastic bottles. Many of the stairs had gaping holes.

'I don't want to go through one of these and end up dead,' Hugh moaned.

Some of the rooms still contained office chairs and tables. Like the rest of the building, they were ripe for the rubbish dump. At last they reached the tenth floor.

A shaft of yellow light glimmered from the last room at the end of the corridor. Winston opened the door and walked inside. Hugh hovered behind him, fists at the ready.

A woman was standing at the window, looking out. As they advanced she turned round. Hugh gasped. She had long legs in high-heeled red shoes, a short skirt and an even shorter smile. Actually it was hard to tell about her smile, because her face was covered with a black gauze scarf.

'Hello, Winston,' she said huskily. 'I had a feeling you might show up.'

'You had? Well, I must say I wasn't expecting you. But it's nice to meet you.' Winston held out his hand. 'Who are you, by the way?'

'You can call me Abacus. But what have you boys been doing? Mud-wrestling?'

Winston shot Hugh an accusing glance. 'This is our casual look,' he murmured.

Hugh stood there, gaping, his hand foolishly outstretched as Abacus strolled back to the window.

'Feel free to stay, boys.' She pointed to the window, where she had a digital camera set up on a tripod. The camera was trained on a window of the hotel opposite. Was this the suite where John Minor was meeting al-Yamani? 'But I'm a bit pushed for time right now. I would appreciate it if you didn't –' Abacus paused and gave a low, throaty chuckle – 'well, ruin the picture.'

The camera was a state-of-the-art digital model. With his excellent long-range eyesight, Winston could see the the picture in the camera's small viewfinder. It was blurred but unmistakable: the interior of a luxury hotel room. On a glass top table there were bottles.

And two champagne flutes.

The woman turned back to the window. Winston spotted her tiny earpiece. There were only two possibilities. Someone was guiding her, or she was listening in to the conversation across in that hotel room. It must be al-Yamani's suite.

Hugh was still staring at Abacus, his mouth hanging open. Typical, thought Winston, one glam woman – even one without a face – and Hugh started behaving like a goldfish. He wouldn't be much good in a fight if a pair of glossy legs deprived him of the use of his wits.

'Can you tell me one thing, Abacus?' Winston asked. 'How do you know who I am?'

The woman sat down on a battered swivel chair and crossed her legs. In the background Hugh gulped some more. 'I have ways of knowing,' she said mysteriously.

'Why are you so interested in that empty hotel room?'

'I've got a lot of interests. I keep bees in my spare time.'

Winston hadn't much hope of getting a straight answer out of her so he changed tack. 'Who do you work for?'

'I'm a free agent.'

'You'll forgive me if I'm not convinced.'

'Forgive me if *I'm* not impressed by the opinions of a twelve-year-old,' Abacus replied sweetly.

Winston ignored the gibe. 'The earpiece is a bit of giveaway. You're being *directed* by someone.'

Abacus's hand shot to her ear. 'Rubbish!' The woman's voice had risen. Now it was no longer husky, it was shrill. Winston guessed that somehow he had scored a hit. 'Listen, kid, I'm in charge here. I think it's time you learned some manners.'

Across the car park, in the Hampton Village Hotel, figures entered the mysterious empty room. Winston could make out a man wearing a white headdress. And another man. Too blurry to see clearly.

Abacus fiddled with the camera – and in the view-finder a little tableau sprang into life. John Minor with a champagne glass in his hand, the mother of all grins on his face. And another man in an Arab robe and headdress.

Quickly Winston scanned the face for similarities. Yes, he was ninety-eight per cent certain the man was al-Yamani. The blurring of the original MI5 photo left some doubt, but very little. Winston would have recognised those canines anywhere.

John Minor was happy. He waved his hands

around. Al-Yamani popped the cork on the bottle of champagne. Minor held out his glass and had it filled with bubbly. He laughed. Even without sound you could tell he was laughing. A lot. He put his head back and tossed the champagne down in one gulp.

Al-Yamani toasted John Minor and drank his health. Then he disappeared, returning with a brown suitcase, which he opened. It was full of money. Stacks and stacks of pound notes, like you see in gangster films.

John Minor took out one of the notes and kissed it. He put it back in the suitcase. He closed the case and picked it up.

Winston had seen enough.

'Hugh,' he said, 'if you don't mind. Get me the memory card from the camera.'

Abacus took one look at Hugh and burst out laughing.

'If you make trouble my bodyguard will handle it,' Winston said. He felt justly proud of Hugh, hulking in the doorway in his black leathers. 'I'm afraid you stand no chance against him.'

'You naughty boy.' Abacus forced the words out through her giggles. 'You really will be the death of me.' With a quick flick of her legs, she threw her red stilettos off and caught them in her dainty hands. Then she turned to Hugh, whose fists hung uselessly at his sides.

'I really don't fight ladies,' he said. 'Sorry. Bad manners.'

'I don't fight schoolchildren. Hey, let's both make an exception.'

'Very well. Queensberry rules and all that.' Reluctantly, he raised his fists. 'No seconds, wrestling or, erm, ahem –' Hugh turned a rich plum colour – 'hugging.'

But Abacus wasn't listening. She advanced on Hugh. One wallop from her stilettos sent him down. She knelt over his body and dealt him a couple of quick blows.

Then she got up to deal with Winston.

This was no time for scruples. Winston overcame his own distaste for physical effort and grasped one of the swivel chairs, shoving it at Abacus. It caught her on the shins. She fell backwards, landing with a thump on the tiled floor. Winston had a momentary flash of her face. Lush lips, gappy teeth, wide cheekbones. He filed away the image. Quickly he opened up the camera and pocketed the memory card.

'Come on, Hugh!' Winston gave his comatose

sidekick a good shake. 'For goodness' sake.'

'Whhaaat . . . ****@@@??' the bodyguard spluttered.

Winston dragged him up by the scruff of his neck and stood him on his feet. 'Get up, you useless lump. She'll come to in a second.'

Blearily Hugh followed Winston towards the stairs. Ten floors later, they ran out on to the forecourt. Glancing up, Winston saw Abacus watching them from a balcony. She had a mobile phone pressed to her ear.

Hugh jumped on the bike and revved it up. As Winston climbed on behind him, a blue Mercedes drove into the road in front of them, blocking their path. A dark figure was getting out of the passenger door. A dark figure carrying something. Some kind of weapon.

'What the hell?' Hugh said.

'Forget it. Just drive,' Winston yelled.

Even in an emergency, Hugh looked after his friend. 'Aren't you forgetting something?' he shouted, pointing to Winston's head.

'What?'

'Your helmet.'

'Drive. Damn it.'

Winston was generally safety-conscious, but this time he was going to put life before limb.

As the bike raced towards the blue Mercedes, the man pointed the weapon at them and pulled the trigger. Winston had a flash of his face in the bike's headlights. As well as his teeth. They were embossed with tiny diamonds, L-O-V-E at the top, H-A-T-E at the bottom. Hugh squeezed the accelerator and the Harley took flight, skimming straight towards the car.

The last thing Winston saw before he closed his eyes was a glittering black harpoon, released from the gun, and it was coming straight for him.

It didn't look like the kind of missile that would take no for an answer.

CHAPTER TWELVE

'It could be a stitch-up. Minor was in the wrong place at the wrong time.' As soon as he said the words, Winston knew they were unconvincing.

The image of John Minor taking a stack of money out of a suitcase and kissing it played across the computer screen. Winston and Hugh knew there was no mistake. Minor was kissing a wad of dosh. Their usual roles were reversed. Winston was being the nice guy, trying to find every possible excuse, while Hugh played the cynic. Or the realist.

'Right, and he kissed that wad of money by mistake,' Hugh said. 'Or maybe you think that's Minor's double?'

'No. That's John Minor. There's no way they could have replicated his teeth, and look at his ear. He's got a very distinctive lobe. I mean, even with plastic surgery . . . no, that is John Minor.'

'Then he's sunk. He's a crook.' Hugh was the kindest person Winston knew, but when someone did something really wrong he was uncompromising. 'He should be locked up in prison.'

It was the evening of the next day and Winston and Hugh were sitting in Hugh's attic bedroom, rewatching the stolen footage, trying to spot clues. They were exhausted after their ordeal. In fact Winston had to keep pinching himself to prove he was alive. It had taken a miracle to get away from the thugs with the harpoon. If Hugh had let them down against Abacus, he had more than redeemed himself on the bike. He had driven like a human typhoon. They'd thundered straight at the blue Mercedes. Ahead of them the heavy pulled the trigger and the harpoon gun came at them, missing their heads by a whisker. A split second later Hugh had ramped the car and the boys went whizzing through the air.

It had helped that the motorbike seemed to sprout wings midair. One of GQ's little innovations.

They came down with a bone-crunching thud. Winston's neck jerked forward and thumped into Hugh's back. As he was struggling to stay on the bike,

Hugh hit a button with his head and a missile flared out of the bike's rear. It zoomed across the ground, just missing the thugs. But the missile gave them a few seconds of surprise as the chasing car veered to the left. And they were away, driving madly across the fields.

Away! With the memory card.

Now Winston was trying to work out what to do with it. Every time he saw the stolen footage he felt sick to his stomach. But he still didn't want to rush to judgement. He prided himself on reacting to problems with his head, not his guts.

'Let's go for a walk. I need some air. I'll take the memory card,' he said, slipping it into his left sock.

'Why?' Hugh asked, 'It'll be fine here.'

'I don't want you losing it. I expect if Abacus came calling you'd just give it to her.'

'Unfair,' said Hugh grumpily.

They strolled past the River Thames and into the West End. There wasn't much traffic these days, even at rush hour. The cars that were on the road were often crammed to bursting. A red double-decker passed them and Hugh suggested getting on, but Winston shook his head. He didn't fancy fighting for space with all the people hanging off the sides of the bus.

Then they were in the heart of theatreland and Hugh was aahing over the lavish showbiz posters. Winston ignored him, deep in thought.

Suddenly Winston stopped in front of a poster, eyeing it thoughtfully. 'Let's go and see this tonight,' he suggested.

'*The Sound of Music*. Great,' Hugh replied.

The poster showed two actors holding hands against a backdrop of mountains.

'But listen. Um, could you lend me the money?' Hugh muttered. 'Tickets are expensive and I've –'

'It's OK. I'll treat you.'

'I couldn't.'

'Look, I insist. You saved me from being speared by a harpoon, the least I can do is buy you a theatre ticket.'

The show was not popular. Winston queued at the Gaiety Theatre box office and bought two front-row tickets. He had just paid when he felt a tap on his shoulder. It was Sir Giles, accompanied by his son and Lady Lushington. Jago glared and Lady Lushington gave him a frosty smile, but Sir Giles was beaming.

'Ah, Winston. I've heard about your friend. You're the boxing champ, I believe.'

'This is Hugh Ray-Chaudhury. He's the best featherweight Duffham has ever had,' Winston said.

'Just as long as they stick to the Queensberry rules,' he added in an undertone.

'Delighted to meet you, Hugh.' Sir Giles smiled. 'You like *The Sound of Music*, do you? It's an odd choice for a couple of young lads, I must say. You must sit with us in the VIP box. My wife insisted I come. Bit of bore, as I'm not a musical fan.'

'Giles, that's a lie. You dragged me here,' Lady Lushington put in crossly.

The couple bickered for a minute. Then the minister turned to the boys and was all charm as they went to take their seats in the Gaiety's VIP box. But Winston couldn't help thinking that the minister was secretly not pleased to see him.

It was a first night, but perhaps because the leads were a couple of unknowns, Clare Ward and Jules Petit, the theatre was far from full. There were a few minor 'celebs'. Winston spotted an actress he knew from somewhere. But on the whole the crowd looked less than excited. And how right they were. When the curtain lifted Winston found himself stuck in one of the most tedious shows he'd ever had to endure.

The Sound of Music had been his sister's favourite film. He'd had a soft spot for it himself. But this production didn't just murder the story, it hung it by the neck, then very slowly had it drawn and quartered.

The VIP box actually had a terrible view of the stage. Winston leaned forward, his eyes glued on the actors. Sir Giles chatted away to Winston about politics and sport throughout the show. At the interval Hugh suggested they go backstage to see if they could meet the stars.

'Stars?' asked Winston, confused.

'You know, Clare Ward and Jules Petit. I might get some tips on how to break into showbiz.'

Hugh was surprised when Winston agreed, but the minister laid a hand on his arm to detain him. While Lady Lushington and Jago went off to the bar, Sir Giles leaned over to Winston and spoke in an undertone. 'Have you had any thoughts since we last spoke, dear boy?'

'One or two. It's been a slow week.'

A strained smile crossed Sir Giles face. 'What? No news on the email you found on John Minor's computer? As you know, the country is close to crisis. Oil is running out . . . The email is . . . political dynamite, Winston. Points to corruption among the highest in the land . . .'

Winston nodded.

'It is your duty to send it the press. You must not

allow a misplaced loyalty to the prime minister to cloud your judgement. Sadly, he doesn't deserve it.'

Winston thought of the scene from the stolen recording. Minor kissing the money while al-Yamani looked on. It was such a crude gesture. The kind of thing a baddie would do in a B–grade movie.

Winston stopped paying attention to the musical in the second half. He closed his eyes for a minute. A fraction of an instant later Hugh was shaking him.

'How could you?' Hugh sounded hurt. 'You missed some gorgeous tunes.'

Winston sat bolt upright, instantly awake. 'The memory card,' he gasped. He leaned down and felt in his sock. It was OK, it was still there. He looked over Hugh for the minister, but Sir Giles was gone. Lady Lushington and Jago were still there, whispering together.

'He said he had to leave. Urgent meeting,' Hugh explained, catching Winston's glance. 'Said he didn't want to wake you.'

'All right. Let's get out of here.'

Outside it was pelting with rain and the streets were crowded with soggy people. Winston and Hugh blended in with the masses, making for the tube, when a minicab pulled up beside them.

'Wanna ride, sir?' said the driver. 'Very cheap.'

'No thanks,' Winston said, walking on.

'You'll get soaked, mate. A fiver to Westminster.'

Winston's heart missed a beat. 'Run for it,' he shouted to Hugh.

'What? Why?' Hugh was bewildered.

'How does he know where we live? RUN!'

Too late. Winston felt a gun poking into his ribs.

'Get in,' a man grunted.

Winston was too smart to argue with guns. He got into the cab, with Hugh coming after him.

'What the hell is going on?' Hugh sputtered. But even Hugh didn't really need to ask.

Expert hands frisked them. A goon found the memory card in Winston's sock. Winston saw the glint of diamonds shining in the dark interior of the man's mouth.

'It's empty. You won't get anything –' But his words were cut off. A cloth was placed over his mouth and nose. He tried not to inhale the vapour coming off the material. Its smell was rich and sickening.

Chloroform.

CHAPTER THIRTEEN

Ouch.

Winston tried to ungum his eyelids. They were stuck together with gluey muck. He shuffled on the floor and pain flooded through him. When he moved he took Hugh with him.

The two were tied together with thick garden twine, piled like bundles of rubbish in the back of a shed. Both boys' hands and feet were tied together. Light was shining through gaps in the wooden-plank walls. The illuminated dial on Winston's watch said 4.45 a.m. Winston had no idea how long they'd been out. The DVD recording of John Minor and al-Yamani was gone. And so was the printout of the email which Winston had found on Minor's computer.

Hugh was breathing heavily through his open mouth.

'Wake up,' Winston said, poking him in the ribs.

Hugh grunted in his drugged sleep and moved over, causing Winston to roll with him.

'Wake up, you idiot. We've gotta get out of here before those heavies come back.'

Winston rolled on to Hugh's stomach, digging his bound hands into his ribcage, but the boxer slept peacefully on. It was going to take a ten-ton truck to wake him up. Winston somehow manoeuvred his hands over Hugh's mouth and blocked his air supply. Then he pinched his nose. The boxer gurgled and opened one eye. When he saw Winston's furious face, inches from his own, he suddenly jerked wide awake.

'What's up?'

'We're on holiday in Majorca. What do you think? We're tied up in a shed and those psychos could be back any minute. Let's get out of here.'

'How?' Hugh held up his hands, which were bound with triple sailor knots. 'These are impossible to get out of. You'd have to be Houdini.'

'Still got your lighter?'

Hugh nodded. 'I can feel it in my shirt pocket. But I can't get it out.'

'Let me have a go.'

'What do you want it for? You don't want to burn down the shed.'

'Never mind.'

Winston managed to ease the lighter out of Hugh's pocket with two fingers. It was an old-fashioned army model that snapped on when you opened the top. He'd just managed to raise a flame when he dropped it. Laboriously he got the lighter into position again between his legs and flicked the lid. The flame was long and hot. Winston held his bound hands over it.

'Don't do it.' Hugh winced.

The rope shrivelled and burned. And so did the bottom of Winston's right hand.

'I'm going to be sick,' Hugh moaned.

'Excuse me,' Winston said between gritted teeth. 'This is my hand after all.'

He shook the rope to the floor in a blaze of flames and jumped on it. Pain filled his head but he willed it away. He untied his legs. And then he turned to Hugh, blinking away the tears in his eyes.

'Does it hurt?' Hugh was looking at his friend with a new expression: half awe, half fear.

'Of course,' Winston snapped. 'But I bet what

those men would do to us would hurt a teeny bit more. Come on.'

The door was locked. Winston got busy with the inner tube of the biro he always carried for lock-picking. Hugh couldn't drag his eyes away from Winston's raw, blistering hand. Within seconds the door creaked open. Winston collected his digital organiser and jacket, which were in a heap by the door, and they stepped out into a garden. Dawn was breaking. Birds were twittering and they could see a cat slinking through some bushes.

They climbed over the fence into the garden next door and then over another fence till they came to a high wall. Once over that they were in a quiet, tree-lined road. Nobody was up yet, so the place was deserted.

'Haven't a clue where we are,' said Hugh as they walked fast towards the sound of traffic.

'Holloway.'

'You been here before?'

'No, N19. On that street sign. Postcode for Holloway.'

'Honestly, you are such a nerd sometimes.' Hugh smiled at his friend affectionately. 'Where do you put it all?'

Winston ignored him. 'We'd better buy the papers.

See if those crooks have sold the recording.'

They had emerged on to a big motorway, near a flyover bridge. A few cars were driving down into London and there was a paper seller near the tube. Hugh bought copies of all the dailies. The two boys rifled through them in the half-deserted street, while the newspaper vendor looked on as if they were barmy.

Winston found it hard to concentrate. His head was heavy, his eyes sticky and his mouth felt like an unflushed toilet. That was nothing compared to how his hand felt, stinging as if a thousand needles were pressing into his flesh. Still, he knew there was no need to look in the papers too closely. If the press had had the story of the PM and the oil billionaire, it would have been splashed across the front page.

'There's nothing here,' Hugh said. 'Total washout.'

Perhaps the thief didn't want to sell the footage to the press. Perhaps, Winston thought, they wanted to blackmail the PM. Or had some other sinister motive.

'You should get that hand seen to,' said Hugh, noticing how pale his friend looked. 'Look, there's a hospital just up the road. I'm taking you. If you don't have it looked at, you may get gangrene.'

'I doubt it. Penicillin has seen off gangrene.'

'Something equally horrible then. We're going. Now.'

Unwillingly, Winston let himself be guided to the hospital, where they joined a few drunks and the frantic-looking parents of a screaming baby in the dingy waiting room.

Wake Up, Britain was jangling through its theme tune on a TV in the corner. Winston glanced at the screen in a bored way and something hit him like a shotgun in the chest. Ricky and Kath weren't smiling. Ricky and Kath were always smiling. Their smile was as much a part of the show as Ricky's perma-tan and Kath's blonde highlights.

'This is one of the gravest days in *Wake Up, Britain*'s history,' said Kath, looking very sombre. 'Exclusively on *Wake Up, Britain* today we will reveal the scandal that could bring down the government. A year ago John Minor met Ricky and they swapped football stories.'

A picture of a smiling John Minor flashed up on screen – on the famous apricot-coloured couch with an oh-so-smiling Ricky.

'Today John Minor stands accused of selling Britain's national interests down the river in return for a suitcase of cash,' Kath continued.

The TV cut from the studio to the grainy footage of the clandestine recording. There was John Minor, red-faced and genial, taking that suitcase from al-Yamani.

Winston glanced at Hugh. He looked stricken.

Then Ricky's face was back on screen, grinning again. 'And later Kath will be meeting makeover expert Tricia Pout. The lovely Ms Pout will be explaining how to take ten years off your age for just ten pounds.'

Winston had seen enough.

'I've gotta go,' he said, getting up.

'You can't,' Hugh said firmly.

Winston had no time for full sentences. 'Parliament. Can't miss.'

He was already out of casualty, melting into the crowds of sick people in the main hospital. Hugh ran after him, shouting frantically.

'Your hand, Winston. They'll survive without you, but you'll never get another hand.'

But Winston had gone.

CHAPTER FOURTEEN

MPs gathered like pinstriped vultures, eager to be there at the kill. Even those who rarely made it in before tea time were huddled in tight knots in the doorways and corridors – all talking in excited whispers.

Winston headed straight for the canteen, the hub of parliamentary gossip. If you wanted to know the latest rumours, this was the place to be. While he was there he stocked up on calories: eggs, beans, bacon, hash browns, four pieces of toast. Strange how a full stomach made the dull throb in his right hand less painful. He was just washing it all down with a mug of warm milk when Dame Stella Curry came into sight, like an oil tanker in a platinum wig. She was accompanied by a young man, her secretary maybe.

Dame Curry was nearly six foot in her silk

stockings. Her hair stood in stiff, cardboard waves and her neck was loaded with a bicycle chain of glistening pearls. Being leader of Her Majesty's official opposition party, Dame Curry was far too grand to waste her time chatting to schoolboys. But the whole of Parliament knew that Winston had become a sort of government mascot.

So Dame Curry condescended. 'Well, *my little man –*' She grinned, stopping by Winston's table with a tray that contained everything he had on his plate PLUS sausages, pancakes with maple syrup and half a packet of cheese. 'Looks like your days here are numbered. Back to school for you, and a jolly good thing too, I should think.'

'I can't return to school at present.'

'Think you're too good for it now, do you? Fancy yourself as one of the big boys?'

'It's the summer holidays, Dame Curry.'

'All right, smarty-pants,' Dame Curry replied. For a hideous moment, Winston thought she was going to ruffle his hair. 'Well, you should be off with the Boy Scouts or something then. Not bothering with grown-up business.'

They were interrupted by the national anthem: Dame Curry's mobile phone ringtone. 'Business calls, boyo.' She answered the phone. 'Of course, Jeremy,' she barked. 'Always happy to do an interview with the *Tommorrow* programme. I'll be even happier to do interviews with you lot when I'm PM . . . Ha ha ha ha ha,' she laughed, showing her chunky molars gleaming with black fillings.

Winston guessed that it was Jeremy Glass, presenter of the radio politics show.

'Well, of course I know,' Dame Curry bellowed in answer to a question. 'It's my job to keep up with the news. This is my statement: "John Minor has no option but to resign. He has been caught with his nose in the trough. Red-handed, you might say. If he has any integrity he should go immediately. Clear the air and prepare the way for a fresh start."'

Dame Curry listened to another question, her wrestler's face quivering with excitement. 'Well, there might be an appointment of course. Sir Giles, I suppose, is the obvious candidate for the next PM. Or Tony Favour, he's been competent if uninspiring at Energy. But I really think we should have an immediate general election –'

She listened again and now she was frowning. 'Yes, I know we've just had an election. No, an election would NOT be a waste of money. This scandal casts doubt on the trustworthiness of the entire party.'

The canteen was full of MPs. They were clustered in buzzing swarms around the coffee machine and the tables. There was an end-of-term atmosphere in the place. The politicians had reacted to the scandal just like the Duffham boys on the day they heard the headmaster had been thrown off his horse and landed head-first in a freshly manured field.

There was a heady smell in the air. Eau-de-excitement. Any change in government, particularly at the top, meant there was hope of going up a few notches on the slippery slope to power.

Winston suddenly had no appetite for the rest of his bacon and eggs. He got up to leave.

Tony Favour, the energy minister, was holding court by the door to the canteen. He couldn't stop the grin which kept spreading across his toothy mouth. 'Terrible news. Terrible,' he was saying to a gnome-like MP, his eyes strafing the room, on the lookout for someone more important to talk to.

Then Favour spotted a lovely assistant and he lit up. 'Ah, Cicely,' he said, putting his arms round her. Winston had already noted that Tony Favour liked to have an audience of well-groomed young women hanging on his every word. 'A very black day. Very sad indeed,' Mr Favour was saying happily as Winston left the canteen.

Winston walked slowly up the stairs to John Minor's office. He showed his security vetting pass to the two guards and the MI5 officer on duty and went into the PM's suite. The PM's secretary was sitting at her desk typing away, her face strained.

In the corner was a bank of flickering TVs. The secretary's eyes kept returning to them. Winston could see a reporter interviewing Dame Curry on one. On another the Ali al-Yamani recording was playing.

Raised voices were coming through the doors from the PM's office. John Minor and his press minder. The PM sounded angrier than he imagined possible.

'It's RUBBISH. A pitiful excuse. It just won't wash, John,' the minder shouted.

'SHUT UP. I AM SICK OF BEING TOLD WHAT TO SAY BY YOU. I AM SICK OF SPIN AND PUTTING THE BEST ANGLE ON THE STORY,' the PM exploded. It was as shocking as hearing a sheep roar. 'I'M NOT GOING TO BE BULLIED BY YOU THIS TIME. I AM GOING TO TELL THE TRUTH.'

'No one will believe you,' the minder said more quietly.

'I don't care. It is the truth and I am going to tell it.' John Minor came charging out of his office and went over to his secretary. 'Get the BBC here,' he ordered. 'NOW.'

'Yes, PM,' she said meekly. Her eyes, Winston noticed, were red-rimmed.

Within seconds a BBC crew had arrived and set up their klieg lights. John Minor sat behind his desk, pictures of his family and the Queen behind him. He looked tired and sad.

'My fellow Britons, what I have to say to you today is straight from the heart. I have always done my very best by you. However silly I have been, I hope you believe that I would never let you down.

'I am accused of a very serious crime. Taking money from Ali al-Yamani, a man who is no friend of this country. I have been caught on film drinking this man's champagne and taking a suitcase of his money.'

John Minor paused and looked deep into the camera. For the first time Winston could see how this nondescript man came to be PM. He wasn't talking to the camera. He was speaking to every person in the country – in their living rooms and offices. He radiated sincerity. If it was acting he deserved an Oscar for his performance.

'On my word of honour, that film is a lie. I have never taken money from al-Yamani and I have never betrayed my country. I believed the man I am now told is al-Yamani to be Ali al-Hadji, the Monopoly champion of the Middle East. He had a very impressive record. So when he challenged me to a match, I accepted. Maybe it would have been better if I had not won.

'Yes, the suitcase I took from this man was full of money. But it was Monopoly money. Pretend money.' Mr Minor looked down and when he looked up again his eyes were watery. 'I have been very foolish. But believe me, my friends, I have never been dishonest.'

CHAPTER FIFTEEN

'John Minor, THE INVISIBLE MAN!' Dame Stella Curry placed her meaty hands on her hips and her backbenchers roared with laughter. 'Are we to be favoured with an explanation for the PM's VANISHING ACT?'

This is what it must have been like at a hanging, Winston thought, back in the days when an execution was the Londoner's favourite day out.

Parliament was packed. Even those elderly, sick or merely lazy MPs who never bothered to make an appearance had come out for the show. Excited whispers ran through the throng. There was muffled laughter.

The only person missing was Sir Giles Lushington.

Winston seemed to be alone in not being excited.

The energy minister, Tony Favour, was making a speech, doing his best to look sad. That was just like him, Winston thought, all doe-eyed sincerity on the outside and malice on the inside. No wonder his nickname was Barbie. 'Spare some sympathy for John Minor and his family, at this bleak moment in his life,' Favour was saying.

Winston noticed a growing stir among the journalists on the press benches. Several were whispering. Others were listening to their headphones or watching the news on their digital organisers. Discreetly Winston inserted his earphones and switched on to the twenty-four-hour rolling news channel on his own digital organiser. A wobbly video filled the screen.

Back in Parliament Dame Curry was still on the warpath.

'My friend Tony asks us to spare John some sympathy! All I'd spare him is a spell in prison.' Dame Curry paused and the chamber exploded with laughter. She continued, 'The last thing we politicians should do is to make fools of ourselves by clinging to power when we've been shown up. It destroys the public's trust in us.'

Winston stood up and caught the Speaker's eye.

The Speaker nodded, indicating he could go next.

'I have a question for the honourable lady.'

'I can't take a question from a juvenile. It's not dignified,' Curry boomed. 'That kid shouldn't be here.'

Some MPs shouted that he should be given a chance and the public gallery booed and hissed.

'Objection,' the Speaker shouted, banging his gavel on the table. 'Disrespect. The young gentlemen is here as our guest.'

When she saw she'd slipped up, Dame Curry, terrified of being unpopular, immediately relented.

'Dame Stella Curry, if you were caught on film taking a gift from Ali al-Yamani would you resign?' Winston asked.

'What a ridiculous question! I would never behave inappropriately.'

'Please answer the question.'

'I don't deal in make-believe, young man. I deal in facts.'

'Answer the question.'

'Well, I can't. I've never met al-Yamani.'

'Answer the question.'

'I'm always one hundred per cent honest. That is why no one has ever called for my resignation.'

'Has being a politician made you unable to answer

a simple question? WOULD YOU RESIGN if you were caught taking a present from al-Yamani? It's a question any *juvenile*, as Dame Curry calls us, could answer.'

There was silence. Then people began to laugh. Mostly at the expression on Dame Curry's face.

'Turn on the telly. I promise you there's something good on for a change,' Winston shouted above the laughter.

The Speaker banged the gavel again and shouted, 'Order, order. Not possible. It is totally against parliamentary traditions.'

But somebody had already unrolled a flexible television. What the MPs saw on the plasma screen left them – for once – silenced.

Dame Curry, glowing in a lime-green suit, was shaking hands with Ali al-Yamani. They seemed to be in a car park, standing next to a blazing red Ferrari. The newsflash at the bottom of the screen revealed that the Ferrari was hand-built and costs five times Dame Curry's annual salary.

'Jolly good, Ali. I've always wanted my own Ferrari,' Dame Curry joked. Then al-Yamani handed her the keys to the car and, with an inelegant flash of her knees, a broadly smiling Dame Curry manoeuvred herself in. Grinning through the windows, she gave a thumbs-up sign. Then, with a rev of the engine, she drove off and the screen faded to black.

The news cut back to the studio and the presenter was asked if this meant the end of Dame Curry's career in politics.

Winston looked from the screen to the real Dame Curry. She was watching the footage, her eyes glazed.

'Cat got your tongue, Dame Curry?' Winston queried cheekily.

CHAPTER SIXTEEN

'Tweet, tweet, tweet.' A riot of twittering and chirruping erupted in the bedroom. Hugh groaned. This was his early-morning novelty ringtone. Sleepily he reached for his mobile.

'Meet me at Elephant and Castle,' Winston hissed, without bothering with greetings. 'Bring the bike. We may need to make a quick getaway.'

'Sure. What's up?'

'Later. See you at the crossroads of Hazel Gardens and Lark Close about 9 a.m. Got it? Make sure you're discreet.'

Winston hung up the phone – he had used a call box in case his mobile was bugged – and joined the commuters waiting for the bus. While he queued his mind went over the newspapers. It was the morning after the scandal had broken and the press had gone bananas.

PM IN SOUP, one headline blared. **STELLA IN CURRY**, screamed another. And in the *Stun*, over a picture of Tony Favour, **BARBIE GOES BELLY UP**.

What? Tony Favour. It couldn't be.

But it was. His famous hair was ruffled, his face smeared with lipstick. He was bending down and removing a diamond from the navel of a bellydancer. In another snap the diamond gleamed between his teeth. In the background was Ali al-Yamani, frozen in the act of clapping.

MORE SLEAZE, roared the paper. Underneath it asked in smaller type, **IS THIS THE STOLEN MILLENNIUM DIAMOND?**

But that wasn't all.

A well-known 'TV personality' MP was snapped having a fist-fight with his 'love rival', a backbencher. Both men looked ridiculous, stripped down to their vests and Y-fronts.

Another MP, who had become well known for his support for healthy eating, was caught in the act of munching his way through a plate of doughnuts: super-sickly ones decorated with pink frosted icing and hundreds and thousands. Hardly the five portions of fruit and veg a day that the MP was known for recommending.

And the al-Yamani email was reprinted, together with the story of how Winston Wright, the well-known schoolboy politician, had spotted it in the PM's dustbin. [You can't always trust newspapers to get the details right.]

An editorial said that trust in politicians had been destroyed. The nation's hopes now rested with the younger generation. With people like the brilliant Winston Wright.

But as he struggled on to the crammed bus, Winston wasn't feeling cheered by the paper's praise.

He realised that John Minor, Dame Curry and the other politicians, even he himself, were all pawns in someone else's game. Winston had gone into this business so he wouldn't be bossed about. But here he was being moved around the board like a chesspiece.

He got off the bus at the underground station, still angry, and found his way to Lark Close. Hugh was waiting, the gleaming red Harley hardly inconspicuous.

'What are we doing?' Hugh demanded.

'Just following a hunch. If you really want to know, it's all in the teeth.'

'Teeth? You what?'

Winston put his finger to his lips and Hugh followed as they turned left into Cedar Gardens, a row of Victorian houses that had been turned into flats. Despite the rustic name, this was one of the most run-down parts of inner London, littered with fast-food cartons and crisp packets. Winston rang the bell at number 28b. When no one answered he put on some thin gloves and got out his biro tube.

'Are you out of your mind?' Hugh hissed. 'Whose flat is this?'

'The lovely Maria. Clare Ward from The *Sound of Music.*'

'We can't burgle her flat.'

'Sshhh.'

Within seconds Winston had picked both the outer lock and the flimsy Yale. But the door wouldn't budge. Both boys leaned against it and it suddenly swung free.

Clare Ward had one of the messiest homes Winston had ever seen. Skirts and trousers, under-wear and make-up were all scattered around the floor, along with dirty dishes and coffee cups. The actress had carelessly left the TV on. Ricky was burbling on about how *Wake Up, Britain* had led the world in exposing political scandal.

'Gross!' Hugh had opened a box of pizza lying next to a glittery skirt. Green mould covered the pepperoni. 'I'm beginning to go off the lovely Miss Ward.'

Winston wasn't listening. He was staring at a mound of furry blankets on the sofa. He gently rolled them over. From under a mass of hair and cloth a face appeared. It was white, lifeless, the crimson-painted lips standing out like a bloody scar.

'We're too late,' Winston said. 'Clare Ward has played her last role.'

CHAPTER SEVENTEEN

'God, I've never seen a dead body before. It's awful,' Hugh said shakily. 'She was just an actress. Who would want to kill her?'

'She got in way over her head,' Winston replied. The dead body lay between them like a reproach. He rolled the body back, covering the terrible white face. 'This is my fault. I should have tried to get her to see sense as soon as I recognised her.'

'What do you mean?'

'Clare Ward was a small-time actress. Then someone approached her and offered to set her up in her own West End show. The catch was she would have to star in some off-stage theatre.'

'So, so she was –' Hugh was struggling to keep up.

'She was Abacus. And Jules Petit, her co-star in

The Sound of Music, played al-Yamani. The guys behind this are pretty efficient. I think we can assume Petit is also dead.' Winston's digital organiser started to beep. He checked it and suddenly his manner became urgent. 'Come on, I want to get over to your place.'

Winston urged Hugh to go faster, even though they were already breaking the speed limit. When they arrived at Hugh's flat he turned on the computer and sat hunched over it without a word.

Finally, Hugh, who had been pacing restlessly about the room, broke the silence.

'I don't understand what's going on, Winston. If you expect me to help you, you've got to fill me in.'

'OK.' Winston sighed, turning his attention away from the computer. 'This whole scandal is a set-up. John Minor, Stella Curry and all the other politicians, they're innocent.'

'Innocent?'

'Yep. One hundred per cent innocent. Someone paid two actors to trap them in a huge political scandal. That someone had a lot of money to spend. Their aim was to bring down the government.'

A glimmer of understanding chased bewilderment

across Hugh's face. 'But who? Who would want to do that?'

'Can't you guess?'

'No.'

'Sir Giles Lushington.'

'But it can't be Sir Giles. I mean, he was your mentor. He was really nice to you.'

'Why?'

'Why what?

'Why do you think he was nice to me?'

'Because he liked you?'

Winston laughed sourly. '*Liking* had nothing to do with it. He used me.'

'How?'

'He needed someone to uncover the scandal and take the heat off him. Someone too young to suspect. Someone everyone would trust.'

'Come off it. I mean, I never really took to Sir Giles, but you think he framed all those people and had those poor actors *killed*?'

Winston sighed. 'He fits the bill in some ways. He's a bitter man. You noticed how he stopped me from going backstage, getting a close look at Clare and Jules.'

'But he let me go backstage.'

'Yep. He took a risk there,' Winston said tactfully.

Hugh flushed. 'So where does that leave us?'

'Pretty much in the dark. We can't prove the actors thing.' Winston turned back to the computer screen. 'Still, there's a glimmer of light in cyberspace.'

Hugh looked over Winston's shoulder at the computer screen. Winston had logged on to a chat room. Something called SmartChat for the High IQ.

'I never thought you'd waste your time talking to loonies in chat rooms. Especially now.'

'This isn't a waste of time. I'm waiting to meet someone.'

'Who?'

Winston stared thoughtfully at the screen. 'Imagine you're rich and powerful. You don't trust the people you work with. Can't stand your family. Have no friends. Who do you speak to? How do you unwind?'

'We talking Sir Giles here?'

'I spotted him a few weeks ago, in the mirror over his desk, using the SmartChat room.'

'Stop doing this to me.' Hugh groaned. 'How could you read his computer backwards in a mirror?'

'It's a doddle. This was Sir Giles's username.' Winston got out a pen and wrote NAM NAC-NAC on a sheet of paper. CAN-CAN MAN.

'I've put a cyberspace tail on his usernamer, so that whenever he enters the chat room I get buzzed. We've been talking quite a bit since then. I think he trusts MOONWALKER more than he trusts the real Winston Wright.'

Hugh stared at the odd nicknames talking to each other in the chat room. 'CAN-CAN MAN's not there, is he?'

'Nope.' Winston tore the packaging off a Kit-Kat, broke it in two and offered half to Hugh. 'I was paged in the flat. He was online and then got interrupted. I hope he'll be back.'

Just then the buzzer on Winston's organiser went off. On the screen the information appeared that CAN-CAN MAN had joined the chat room. Instantly Winston started typing.

MOONWALKER: Hi Can-can man. How R U doing?

CAN-CAN MAN: Had a ruff few days.

MOONWALKER: Me 2. I cld use a whisky.

CAN-CAN MAN: Oh God. Me 2!! In good old days I'd have had dble by now.

'At eleven o'clock in the morning!' Hugh said, shocked.

Winston shrugged and typed.

MOONWALKER: My son's an idiot, he just totalled my Ferarri. My wife wants a new one. Like I'm made of money! How bout U?'

BRAINIAC: Hi i luv Ferraris i can't even afford to drive my Cortina cos petrols so high.

Both Moonwalker and Can-can man ignored the interruption.

CAN-CAN MAN: Thngs R going haywire.

MOONWALKER: Tll me bout it.

CAN-CAN MAN: Where 2 start?

MOONWALKER: Last time we met U said U felt U were walking a high wire.

CAN-CAN MAN: Yeah. I'm being hassled.

BRAINIAC: Wat R U talking bout? Is it my turn to share? I mt learn wire-walking.

CAN-CAN MAN: Gt lost, Brainiac. Tlking to Moonwalker! Moonwalker, can you believe some of the idiots they let into SmartChat.

BRAINIAC: Don't want to talk 2 U. Snob.

BRAINIAC left the chat room.

MOONWALKER: Forget it Can-can man! So who's doing the hassling?

CAN-CAN MAN: No. Don't really know them. Hard to explain. Sometimes I worry I'm not as smart as I think I am. Someone's not being honest with me.

MOONWALKER: Who?

CAN-CAN MAN: Wat?

MOONWALKER: Who is this guy making you do things?

CAN-CAN MAN: Why do U wanna know? Who R U?

MOONWALKER: Forget it. Don't be so touchy. Gotta go.

CAN-CAN MAN: No. Stay. I need 2 talk!

MOONWALKER: See ya round.

CAN-CAN MAN: This same character clls himslf Hope. Fear more like.

MOONWALKER: Hang on. My wife's just walked in.

Winston exited the chat room, leaving Hugh staring at him in perplexity.

'Why do you do that, Winston? You were just getting somewhere.'

His friend smiled. 'I always leave him wanting more, feeling that he wants to earn my trust.'

'Everyone knows you can't trust ANYONE you meet in a chat room,' said Hugh. 'They're full of nutters and people pretending to be someone else. I can't understand how Sir Giles was taken in . . .'

'He's lonely. People do funny things when they're lonely . . . Anyway, I think the time for chat is over. Sir Giles has just grown a tail.'

'Come again?'

'You.'

CHAPTER EIGHTEEN

'What have you got up your sleeve?' Winston asked.

Something glimmered in GQ's hand. 'This beauty was developed last year by our people in Cheltenham. It is virtually undetectable. There are only two other security services that have anything quite so sophisticated: Mossad and the CIA.'

The spook handed Winston a silver box as small as a packet of matches but much slimmer. Flipping it open, he indicated a tiny LCD screen. 'This is a parabolic super-ear. It can track sound from a distance of 490 metres. Through brick walls, concrete and even specially reinforced soundproof rooms. This here is the earpiece.'

'I'm impressed. What do you call it?'

'*We* don't call it anything. RD41, if you want the

technical term. But you can call it a Raspberry if you like. I think that's one of its service nicknames.'

'A Raspberry. I like it. What do I do if I want to tune out background noise and target a conversation? In a restaurant, for example.'

GQ smiled. 'This button here –' he took a small pin out of his pocket and manipulated the miniaturised keyboard – 'brings sound levels up and down. You target the sound you want to bring up like this.'

'It really is dinky. I'm indebted to you, GQ. Before you go, *do* you have a name?'

'Truthfully, it's Lancelot, but I never liked it, and even my mum calls me GQ now . . . Well, be good. Don't do anything I wouldn't do.'

'Doesn't rule much out, does it?' Winston asked with a half-smile as he turned to walk away to the mouth of the alley where Hugh was waiting for him. Then he stopped and peeled a tiny scrap of something off his jacket sleeve.

'I think you might need this,' he said, handing the electronic listening device disguised inside a price tag back to the spy. 'It *is* yours?'

'I've got to hand it to you, your spycraft is impressive for an amateur.' GQ was unashamed. 'Oh, by the way, I've got a different vehicle for you this time. One that blends in more.'

Winston took the keys.

A Granada runabout was waiting for them on the main road. It looked ordinary enough but had been reinforced with a full metal jacket and could withstand up to 2,800 rounds of ammunition.

The boys hid the Granada behind a BritGas van at the corner of Elton Place, waiting for Sir Giles to emerge from his house. They had been there for what seemed like hours when his silver-grey Jaguar drove round to the front of the house and the chauffeur emerged from the car.

'How do we know Sir Giles is going anywhere special tonight?' Hugh asked despairingly. He had been discreetly tailing Sir Giles for two days now and was getting rather sick of the sight of the ministerial Jaguar.

'Just got to hope.'

Sir Giles came out of the house, carrying a leather briefcase. The chauffeur opened the door for him and a moment later the Jaguar was gliding through the Belgravia traffic.

Winston and Hugh followed at a discreet distance. After a while it became clear that the Jaguar was taking an unexpected course into an area where people dumped their rubbish on the streets and left the bins empty. It was hardly the setting you'd expect for the elegant Sir Giles, with his manicured hands and Savile Row suits.

The Jaguar certainly got noticed. In one street a boy threw a stone which bounced off the gleaming paintwork with a clank.

The car was swerving this way and that, as though to dodge a tail. After a while Hugh noticed that a red Ford Cortina that could have been following the Jaguar had been shaken off. Soon after the Jaguar stopped and Sir Giles got out and entered a dingy minicab office.

Some time later he emerged from the minicab office and got into a Renault Espace. The boys followed discreetly as the cab wound its way through scruffy streets to finally stop next to the scattered rubbish of a fruit and veg market.

A neon sign, featuring a pair of boxing gloves, hung over a set of steps that led to a basement door. 'Seconds Out', the glowing yellow letters proclaimed. It was a boxing club. 'Tonight Lousy Lonnie Donegan v. Battling Bubbles Bronco Bullman,' announced one of the posters tacked up outside the club.

The queue to get in snaked all the way down the road to the betting shop on the corner. A bouncer with shoulder-length blond hair checked people as they waited. He seemed to know Sir Giles and let him in with a nod.

'Bubbles?' asked Winston. 'What kind of name is that for a boxer?'

'If you've got a right hook like Bubbles you could be called the Tooth Fairy for all anyone cares,' said Hugh.

'Is he good then?' Winston asked.

'Ace,' Hugh hissed excitedly. 'Lousy Lonnie is a terrific heavyweight.' Then his face dropped. 'They'll never let us in. You don't look eighteen for a start.'

'Let's go round the back,' Winston suggested. 'There might be a service entrance.'

Climbing over a wall, they came into a backyard full of stinking rubbish bins and crates of empty beer bottles. They were in luck. A door was open to the kitchens. They could smell sizzling fat, hear the clink of pans and the shouts of chefs.

'We're going to walk straight through the kitchens and into the club,' Winston instructed Hugh firmly. 'Remember. You belong here. No one will ask any questions.'

He led the way, swaggering through the kitchen. Hugh followed more cautiously.

The kitchen staff were so busy they didn't see the boys, who could have been invisible. A few seconds later and they were through the kitchen and in a dark passage. They emerged in a cavern of an underground boxing club with a ring in the centre, the roped-off space lit by spotlights.

Two boxers were already sizing each other up, circling the ring with their enormous gloved fists, their faces half hidden by their mouthguards.

Around the ring were tables and chairs, where ladies in evening dress drank cocktails and snacked on Mexican food. The boys went round the club discreetly. It was so full of smoke, people and noise that at first they didn't spot Sir Giles.

Winston stopped Hugh with a 'Psst' through his teeth.

'Over there,' he hissed.

Sir Giles was sitting in the shadows with a bald man in a tuxedo. Sweat dripped off his plump nose on to the first of his triple chins. Under his tux his tummy was perfectly round. He looked like a gigantic baby in gangster shades.

Why he needed dark glasses in the dim club, Winston couldn't imagine.

Baby man puffed on a cigar, while Sir Giles drank

a pink cocktail. At the table next to them were three men in black suits. Were they a party of particularly gloomy clubbers? Or were they bodyguards?

Winston chose a table next to the exit. It was smeared with food and held an ashtray with a dozen cigarette stubs. A bored waitress served them. They ordered burgers and chips. The waitress looked surprised when Winston ordered hot milk, but she didn't comment on their age. Then Winston discreetly inserted the earpiece and opened the Raspberry under cover of the table.

At first he just heard a fuzz of magnified noise. He experimented with bringing different sections of the club into focus. With careful targeting, he was able to pinpoint the table of a sleek blonde 100 yards away.

'I always fancied Bubbles,' she was saying. 'He's built like a tank, that one.'

'Naw, you don't know nuffink abaht boxin', babe,' her boyfriend told her patronisingly. 'Lousy Lonnie, 'e looks little but 'e's the one. I'll put a tenner on it.'

Then the bell clanged and the fight began. Bubbles charged at Lonnie and tried to knock him out with a blow to the solar plexus. Lousy Lonnie, surprisingly slight for a heavyweight, performed some pretty nimble footwork. He moved about the ring like a ballerina. He danced and pranced around Bubbles, confounding him with sharp punches.

Hugh was absorbed in the match, but Winston's focus was elsewhere. His surveillance device was now fine-tuned to Sir Giles's table – Sir Giles and the fat baby man. Could he be the mysterious Hope that Sir Giles had mentioned?

'So who do you tip, Brigham? Lonnie?' Sir Giles was asking the fat man.

'He's an unknown quantity. Might make the grade, might not.'

'Bubbles seems in good form.'

Winston heard, but couldn't see, the fat man let out a few puffs of smoke from his cigar. 'Bubbles is getting complacent. And too fat. He needs to lose a few pounds sharpish.'

That was a strange sentiment, Winston thought, coming from someone so super-size.

He couldn't help feeling disappointed. The two men were talking boxing. Perhaps this man Brigham wasn't Hope. Perhaps Sir Giles had travelled to this seedy club, in this run-down neighbourhood, simply to meet a fellow enthusiast of the art of pugilism. But why had Sir Giles taken so much trouble to get to this tatty club far from his usual elegant haunts? With the government about to go up in smoke, surely he had more important things to do than hang out in clubs.

The boys' order arrived. Hugh munched his greedily on his burger, but Winston didn't make much headway with his food. He found that the chewing interfered with the reception in his earpiece. He would have to report the fault to GQ. Agents should be able to eat on stake-outs.

The men were still chatting idly about boxing and clubs. But Winston wasn't taking any chances – he listened to every word.

'Paradise Island, the ultimate holiday destination,' the fat man said.

Winston's ears pricked up. Paradise Island. Wasn't that in the Atlantic Ocean?

'Yes, yes, of course,' Sir Giles said.

'Don't forget. I want it. My own paradise. My stairway to heaven.'

'I'll see what I can do . . .' Winston could hear the unease in Sir Giles's voice.

'No excuses. Just do it. Don't forget, you owe me big time.'

Suddenly Lousy Lonnie gave a high-pitched howl and clutched his ear. Blood was streaming from it.

Battling Bubbles had bitten him. Instantly the

referee rang his bell and all hell broke loose in the club. Customers hooted their disgust. Bubbles was disqualified. 'I declare Lousy Lonnie the winner!' the ref shouted above the mayhem. But Lonnie was in too much agony too care and a stretcher was brought into the ring for him.

'He's an animal, that Bubbles,' Sir Giles said to the baby man.

Babyman puffed on his cigar. 'Yep. A useful one.'

Then the bell clanged and another match featuring some young unknowns began. Most people paid little attention to this contest. Winston decided it was time to make a discreet exit before anything went wrong.

Too late. A very big man had arrived at their table. It was Battling Bubbles Bronco.

When he opened his mouth, he revealed what had been hidden by his mouthguard in the boxing ring. Teeth that were gleaming with the words L-O-V-E and H-A-T-E. Harpoon man.

Bubbles held Hugh by the scruff of the neck and with the other hand reached out to grab Winston. 'Wot you little rats doing 'ere then?'

CHAPTER NINETEEN

'I never miss a good fight.' Quick as a flash, Winston emptied his steaming mug of milk over Bubbles's left hand. 'I love seeing the little guy win.'

The boxer yowled in agony and let Hugh go.

Winston was through the tiny window next to the toilets before Bubbles had finished screaming. Hugh squeezed after him. The boxer tried to follow suit, but he was too big to fit through. The boys clambered through the overflowing dustbins in the club's backyard and over the wall to the alley.

Bubbles came pounding through the back door, just a moment too late. The boys got into their car. Hugh gunned the engine and Winston gave Bubbles a cheery wave out of the armoured windows as the Granada drove away.

'So long,' he yelled.

But he was being optimistic. The heavyweight wasn't beaten yet. Within minutes they spotted Bubbles on the back of a motorbike, a red Mustang. He came after them through the empty streets. Hugh sped out of the seedy suburb, breaking several speed limits. The Mustang stuck to them like a second skin.

'Can't you shake him?' Winston yelled as Hugh crashed a red light, coming within inches of a lorry going the other way.

No luck. The motorbike followed them through.

'Nope,' Hugh yelled. 'He's on a bike.'

And then the traffic slowed. And came to a stop. They were in a jam. A lorry was reversing, blocking the way ahead. They couldn't move. There were buildings on each side and very little pavement.

The motorbike drew up alongside them. Bubbles smiled, his teeth glittering. He drew a knife out of his pocket and slashed the back left tyre – then puttered forward on the bike and did the same with the front.

'A fat lot of good a bulletproof car has been,' Winston hissed.

'Well, you were the one who said a motorbike

wasn't safe,' Hugh snapped back. 'It had to be bulletproof.'

'Nothing's safe when you're being pursued by a maniac.'

There was a silence while the boys faced a grinning Bubbles. Winston wondered if it had been a dentist or a tattooist who decorated his teeth with their charming messages. Bubbles mimed shooting them with his fingers. Then he bent down, picked up the car by the front wheel and lifted it clear off the ground.

'Get out! Make a run for it!' Winston yelled as he crashed into Hugh.

'What about the car? It's worth a fortune. GQ will be furious.'

'Forget the car. Think of your skin.'

Hugh went first, bursting out of the driver's door, which was hanging open precariously in the air. Winston followed him. Around them, people crammed six or seven into a car were watching open-mouthed.

Bubbles put the car down and charged after them. There was a small alley ahead. Bubbles was gaining on them.

They pelted to the end of the road. And then stopped. It was a dead end. Ahead of them rose a block of flats. The door to the flats was locked.

Winston pressed on doorbells. Too late. Bubbles was advancing on them, his mouth a blaze of triumphant light.

'Right, you boyz. Time to sort you out!' he exclaimed. 'Let you get away at the hotel. And the shed. Won't make the same mistake again. Third time lucky.'

He took Winston by the shoulders and lifted him aloft, throwing him from meaty palm to meaty palm. Winston dangled from Bubbles's fists, looking for all the world like a rag doll.

'I can't allow that,' Hugh yelled. He was dancing on the balls of his feet, readying himself for a fight.

Comparing the two boxers, Winston's heart sank. Bubbles looked about twenty stone, while Hugh weighed in at eleven. OK for a featherweight.

Not OK now.

'Come on,' Hugh shouted bravely. 'Do you play Queensberry rules?'

'I PLAY KNOCK YOUR BLOCK OFF!' Bubbles roared. He dropped Winston, who fell flat on his face in the dirt.

With one casual swipe of his mighty fists, Bubbles landed a massive blow to the side of Hugh's chest that knocked his head back with a cracking sound.

But Hugh wasn't beaten. He recovered and

retaliated cleverly, landing a sharp punch on the boxer's neck. It could have been a mosquito bite for all the notice that Bubbles took of it.

Winston judged that it was now time to enter battle. He stuck out his leg and tripped Bubbles up. When he was down, he punched him squarely in the face, trying to knock him out.

'That's not on, Winston,' Hugh rebuked him. 'Not Queensberry.'

'Forget Queensberry. He's gonna kill us.'

The boxer rose from the ground, his nose streaming with blood, spitting out a broken tooth. When he opened his mouth, the appalling extent of his injuries became apparent, for his teeth now spelled L-O-V-E and H-A-T.

Bubbles advanced on the pair of them with a bloodcurdling roar.

'See what I told you?' Winston yelled. 'Do something, Hugh.'

The heavyweight had them cornered against the wall. Winston could feel Bubbles's hot breath on his neck.

'Hugh,' Winston squeaked.

In desperation, Hugh put his head down and charged. His skull got the boxer right in the stomach and he carried him for a foot, before the big man went down with a surprised 'Ouf'. His head landed on the floor with a nasty thud.

Hugh stood over the fallen heavyweight. A lump the size of a golf ball was rising on Bubbles's forehead. 'I don't expect he'll remember anything tomorrow,' he said.

'Well done, Hugh.' said Winston, flicking a speck of dust off his cuff. 'I must admit there was a moment there when I thought you were a goner. Not to mention me.'

'Naw. He was all bone. No brain. Just took a bit of thinking to do him in,' Hugh explained with a smile. The smile was a step too far. Hugh's lip started to bleed freely.

A thoughtful look came over Winston's face as he surveyed the fallen Bubbles and his slightly better-off friend.

'You know, Hugh, you've looked better.'

'This?' Hugh tried to smile again, but his puffy lip stopped him. 'It's nothing.'

'I think you deserve a holiday. You need some beauty sleep. A chance for you to get your looks back.'

'Great. Where we going? Bournemouth?'

'No, somewhere off the beaten track. Somewhere

far away where we can lie low for a bit and take in the local scenery.'

'Wow, the Caribbean?'

'Um, not quite. The place I have in mind is called Paradise Island.'

'Fabulous. I see palm trees, cocktails, a brand-new pair of Bermuda shorts . . .'

CHAPTER TWENTY

The Penguin Arms was decorated with a sign of a penguin carrying a pint in either flipper. When Winston and Hugh walked through the door, conversation in the crowded bar stopped dead – and every pair of eyes in the place swivelled round.

It was like a moment from an old Western when the stranger walks into town.

Their reception in the rest of Paradise Island over the past two days had been just as unfriendly. It had turned out to be a desolate place full of wet sheep and surly islanders. Though it was nearer America than England, the islanders still had the Queen on their postage stamps, and fish and chips and warm beer in their pubs. But they didn't want anything to do with visitors from England, thank you very much. Didn't want anything to do with visitors from anywhere.

Back in the pub the barman looked at the friends as if they were visitors from Mars rather than two schoolboys. 'How old's the kid?' he grunted to Hugh.

'I am not going to drink alcohol. Just milk or a soft drink if you don't have any,' Winston answered.

The publican grunted. Grunts seemed to be a universal language on the island.

Winston had planned his campaign. He wanted to befriend the natives, find out what, if anything, was worrying them. So, after their calamari and chips, he approached the two men at the table next to him and asked if he could buy them a pint.

'I'm from England. I'm here on a school trip doing a project on the culture of Paradise. So I'd be very grateful if you'd have a chat with me and my friend.'

The silence lengthened embarrassingly. The two men stared at Winston. Then the one with a face like an old leather handbag turned to the other. 'I don't think so. Do you?'

'Nah. Bloody spies. We can buy our own pints. Get lost, kiddo.'

There didn't seem to be anything to say to this. So Winston didn't. He retired to his chair by the door, baffled.

Hugh couldn't help smiling. It wasn't often that Winston was taken down a peg or two. But when he saw his friend's expression, his grin turned to sympathy.

'Why are they so unfriendly?' he wondered.

'I'm beginning to think it's my face.' Winston shrugged. 'All the things I read before I came here said how hospitable the locals are. Apparently crime is unknown . . .'

'Some travel guides are rubbish. It's nothing to do with you, Winston. They just hate strangers. It's like that in some of these far-off places. They're hicks. They don't like anyone or anything new.'

'No. It's something else.'

'What?'

'Haven't you noticed something strange?'

'Where do you want me to start? These people are practically cross-eyed with strangeness!'

'No, I don't mean that. The front door of the pub, it has a Fishbein turbo lock.'

'What's that?'

'Fishbein Turbos are handmade by craftsmen in Geneva. Absolutely unpickable. They cost hundreds of pounds a pop . . . and a lot of the windows have iron bars on them. Why would you import a lock from Switzerland? Unless you were scared out of your wits?'

Why indeed? Hugh had no answer. He looked around the pub at the brawny men in T-shirts and shirtsleeves. Their wind-mottled, wary faces glowed in the firelight as they downed their beer. He had thought their expressions were the result of an innate hatred of outsiders. But could he have got them wrong? Might it be fear he saw written in their frowns, not hostility?

By ten o'clock a jet-lagged Hugh was propping up his eyelids with his fingertips, while Winston discoursed on how they would crack the islanders.

'Staying in the Penguin Arms is the most practical way of gaining the psychological advantage,' he said. 'Alcohol loosens people's tongues. We could profit by a loss of their inhibitions.'

'I know you probably read that in a book, Winston, but this is real life.'

'Have you got any better ideas?'

But Hugh's wasn't listening. He'd remembered that he hadn't shown Winston what he'd found earlier that day when he'd gone on a trip to see the island's famous Gentoo penguins.

'Here's what I found on Boulder Beach. They'll be

great for my collection.' Hugh had got his backpack out and taken out some rocks. He put them on the table, next to the remains of his calamari. Some were bluish, some greenish, and all were covered with mud. They left a dirty smear on the tablecloth.

Several eyes around the pub were watching them. Winston stared at the mucky rocks in distaste. 'Do you mind putting your pebbles away. We'll probably get chucked out of here for getting the tablecloth dirty.'

Suddenly a skinny man with grey hair down to his shoulders ran into the middle of the pub. His skin was pitted and scarred with purplish blotches. 'You sit here like drunken sheep and the sacred spell is broken. Evil voodoo,' he shouted, his Adam's apple jumping around in his thin neck. 'Our land ruined, the purple bull awoken – his rage will kill us all – aaaagggghhh . . .'

'Shut up, Charlie,' the publican yelled.

'The evil eye is upon us,' Charlie frothed. He turned and pointed a quivering finger at Winston and Hugh. 'Do not play with fire. The land whithers and dies. Evil voodoooooooooooo.'

A couple of islanders rushed up to stop Charlie, who was now trying to take his clothes off.

'He's a sick man,' a woman spat at Hugh and

Winston. 'Shame on you for watching. SHAME ON YOU.'

Charlie had already managed to take off his trousers and jumper. But strong hands grabbed him and, wrapped in a tablecloth, he was escorted into the back of the pub.

Shortly after that Winston gave in to Hugh's demands and they walked wearily down Adam Street towards their hotel.

'That was spooky,' Hugh said.

Winston nodded, looking thoughtful. 'They're very scared. And it looks like they're scared of –'

'Voodoo,' Hugh butted in, shivering.

'Their fear certainly seems to have a supernatural element.'

As they reached their hotel a Land Rover drove up beside them and screeched to a stop. A big man wearing a scarf over his face got out of the car and barred their way on the narrow pavement. Muscles rippled under his tight sweater like hungry snakes.

'You are Winston Wright,' The man said. It sounded like an accusation.

'I don't deny it,' said Winston. 'In fact occasionally I'm proud of it.'

The man removed the scarf from his face. It was

the policeman Winston had met while Hugh was on his nature trip. 'I know all about you. I have been reading about you in the English papers.' He thrust a rolled-up copy of the *Crusader Digest* at Winston. On page three, under a flattering photo of Winston, was this story:

STILL NO SIGN OF MISSING HERO

MI5 has joined in the hunt for missing schoolboy politician Winston Wright, as concern for his safety grows.

Wright, who disappeared three days ago, won fame for his sharp interventions in Parliament and played a major role in the unmasking of the Ali al-Yamani scandal, which threatens to bring down the government.

There are fears that Wright has been kidnapped by Ali al-Yamani. Reliable sources contacted by the *Crusader* suggest that the schoolboy may have been snatched to prevent him from blowing the whistle on more scandals.

There are concerns that Wright, who is still only twelve, underestimated the

ferocity of the plotters around the Arab sheikh.

Yesterday Sir Giles Lushington, who has been a mentor to the brilliant schoolboy, made an emotional appeal for him to be returned to his family unharmed. 'Winston Wright is a genius, a young boy of exceptional gifts who will be a fantastic asset to this country in the future,' he said. 'I pray that wherever he is no harm will come to him.'

Both MI5 and Scotland Yard stated that they had no suspicions of foul play.

From her modest flat in Borking, Winston's mother, Mrs Shirley Wright, a school dinner lady, seemed confident that her son was all right. 'Winnie's too smart to get caught by bad people,' she said. 'He phoned me several days ago and said he wouldn't be around for a while. But he told me I wasn't to worry. So I'm not. I always do what Winnie tells me.'

Winston supressed a sigh of irritation at the name Winnie. When would his mum learn? He met the policeman's eyes. They were unfriendly.

'What are you doing here? Don't give me any baloney about a school trip. You're trouble.'

Winston decided to give charm one more go.

'Some people *do* think I'm trouble. Not you, I hope. I'd like us to be friends.'

'Get in then.'

The policeman opened the back door of the car and motioned to them. The boys exchanged looks. Winston nodded and they climbed in.

They were in for a shock. There were three big, dangerous-looking men squashed inside the Land-Rover: two in the front, one in the back. Before they realised what was happening, a man got out of the front seat and climbed in after Hugh.

Three men, their faces shielded by dark balaclavas. Three not very chatty men.

The boys were prisoners. The policeman floored the accelerator and the car shot forward, its powerful engine roaring through the stillness of the night.

Suddenly things had got scary again.

CHAPTER TWENTY-ONE

Winston sat in the darkness of his blindfold and a terrible feeling swept over him. It wasn't just fear. Of course he was scared, but this was worse. He was also wrong. Winston *hated* to be wrong.

How could he have been so stupid? The islanders' were clearly in the enemy's pay. And now he had delivered himself and Hugh – trussed up like a couple of turkeys ready for Christmas – into their hands. How could he have been so trusting? So naive? Yes, it had to be faced, so STUPID?

'I hashtoput yoshu to any inconvenienceboyshs but I'm dying for a pee,' Winston said through his gag.

All anybody heard was a muffled mumble.

'There are three of you and two of us,' Hugh put in. 'You have guns and we're unarmed. You don't need to tie us up as well. And you don't need to gag my friend.'

The men didn't bother to reply.

'He'll keep quiet,' Hugh went on bravely. 'Well, he might if you ask him really *nicely*.'

The only answer was the thrum of the engine. After a time Winston heard the sound of the road change. They'd come off the smooth main road a while ago and had been going along rutted country tracks, but now they had begun to bump upwards over a gravel path.

At last the engine came to a stop.

Winston and Hugh could hear the sound of the men unlocking the doors. But all they could see were glimmers of light at the edges of their blindfolds. The doors were locked again. Then they heard footsteps crunching on the gravel. The sound of the men walking away.

The boys were alone in the car.

'What the hell are we going to do?' Hugh asked.

'Mufummeeffe,' Winston mumbled. 'Waff a min.'

He undid the string that the men had used to bind his wrists, using his thumb to unpick the tight knots. In a couple of seconds he was free and had ripped off his gag and his blindfold. Then he tore off Hugh's blindfold and undid the knots that bound his hands.

'They'll be back in a minute, so let's get out of here,' Winston muttered.

'Where are we?'

'How on earth should I know? In the highlands somewhere.'

Winston took out the trusty biro. The Land Rover door was double-locked from the outside. It was just an ordinary lock, however, and so no match for his skill. In a second he had opened it and they were out. The moon shone on soggy turf, rocks and mud. They were in the highlands, far from the sea. Deep in the rough, deserted heart of Paradise.

Too late! The policeman was returning, and behind him his heavy with the Glock pistol glinting in his hand. Hugh slowly put his hands up in the air and Winston followed suit as the policeman angrily shouted at his thugs for letting them go free. A thug put his pistol in Winston's back and the boys were marched into a farmhouse.

It was a large timber-framed building with a roof of rusty tin. It looked abandoned, with weeds growing wild over the front steps. The building radiated a sinister innocence. Were they to be shot and dumped in this lonely spot?

Winston and Hugh were sat down and tied to chairs by the legs, arms and around their waist. One of the men was about to tie another gag around Winston's mouth when their leader ordered him off. The coarse purple string was wound so tight it bit into their skin. The men stood silent while their leader fetched a bowl of water and a knife. Winston had gone light-headed with fear. Besides him he heard Hugh coughing.

'Should I be making my last will and testament?' Winston enquired. 'Leaving the silver spoons and my collection of comics to the grandkids?'

There was no answer to his gag. Trussed up besides him, Hugh groaned.

No one in the whole world knew where they were. There was no hope of rescue. Winston cursed himself for leading them into danger. The sick feeling in his stomach told him how stupid he had been. It was one thing to play with his own life, another to put Hugh's at risk. Why hadn't he just told GQ of his suspicions? Why was he always so foolishly arrogant? And why did he have to make bad jokes when he knew it wasn't a joking matter?

The boss thug walked towards Winston, the sheathed knife dangling from his hand. 'Who are you?'

'Winston Wright, as you know. And this is my friend Hugh Ray-Chaudhury.'

'Didn't I make myself clear?' The thug drew the knife out of the sheath and lovingly ran his finger over the blade. It was very sharp. 'Who do you work for?'

'No one,' replied Winston. 'I've done work experience for the Prime Minister – and Sir Giles Lushington. But I'm not really old enough to have a paid job. British laws prevent child labour, tiresomely.'

'I'm bored of this wise-guy act.' The man sighed. With a quick flick of the knife he slashed at Winston's hand, which was still pink from the lighter burn. A thin cut opened on the skin, blood oozing from it.

Winston screamed once. Then bit back the pain. But his reaction was nothing to Hugh's. The minder began to roar as if his own hand had been slashed.

'Shut up,' the thug snapped at Hugh. Turning to Winston, he commanded, 'What are you playing at? Tell me the truth or I'll kill you.'

Winston tried to hold up his hands in a gesture of surrender. But it was no good, he couldn't lift them away from the chair. He wasn't going to try to be clever. He had the awful, flat feeling that nothing he said or did was going to make much difference now.

'We work for no one. We're just two schoolboys.

There have been odd things in London and we thought Paradise was connected. We don't know how. Or why. But –'

The man didn't let him finish. He turned away from Winston and thwacked Hugh around the face.

Winston's blood boiled. Rage welled up in him. If he was going to go, he might as well go fighting.

'You dirty fool,' he yelled, and charged at the thug, taking the chair with him.

Hugh screamed and followed.

And then the strangest thing happened. Though Winston and Hugh were nowhere near him, the man slipped sideways and fell.

The earth had moved.

A section of the ground now lifted upwards and out of it came a head.

CHAPTER TWENTY-TWO

'Hold it, Joe,' the head ordered.

'Mind your own business, Lucy,' the thug – Joe – snapped back.

'This is my business.'

'This is man's work, little lady.'

'Beating up kids? Joe, these boys are so scared they'll tell you anything you wanna hear.'

'But I was getting somewhere.'

'Not like that,' Lucy insisted. 'We'll end up as bad as them.'

The girl had dirty hair and black eyes. It was as if a wild animal had come crawling out of the trapdoor in the floor. Joe started up again, justifying himself, but the girl cut him off.

'I'm starving.'

She was wearing a filthy yellow jumper and her feet were bare. She levered herself through the trapdoor with one hand, while in the other she was holding a pistol.

One of the men opened a plastic bag with some Tupperware inside. Lucy prised off the lid and a rich smell mixed with the dust in the shack. Stew and a hunk of bread. Everything froze. Using the bread to scoop up the stew, the girl crammed it into her mouth. Within seconds she had eaten the whole container and was licking the edges.

'OK, have it your own way. You wanna take over?' Joe said when she'd finished eating. His manner to her was surprisingly respectful. 'Are these the men?'

The girl walked round Winston and Hugh once. Then she walked round them again.

'Nope.'

'Are you sure?'

'I'm not stupid. The tall one, he is too big. And besides, his face is too . . . too nice. These weren't the guys who came for Pop.'

'You can't be sure. What with everything that happened.'

'Don't patronise me,' Lucy snapped. 'These are little kids. The other guys were built like dumpsters.

I'm telling you, I have never seen these boys before in my life.'

'Well, they've been behaving suspiciously,' Joe said. 'Asking questions. Snooping. I dunno what to do with them.' He changed tack. 'Please come back with me. Mary's been begging me, so have the kids.'

'And what if *they* come back for me?'

'Hah. They'll never get past me.' Joe's hand strayed to his knife.

'Sure, Joe.' The girl looked at him coolly.

'You know, I've kinda learned to rely on myself.' She fingered her gun. 'I fire a pretty straight bullet.'

Winston coughed politely. 'Er, excuse me. Could someone untie us, if we're not the guys you're looking for?'

Both switched their attention to Winston.

'Who are you?' Lucy asked.

'My name is Winston Wright. I'm here to find out how Paradise fits in with some –'

'Cut the crap. You're just a kid,' Lucy butted in. 'What the hell are you doing here?'

'So are you.'

'What?'

'Just a kid. You look about nine to me.'

'Hah, some kid. Anyway, I'm eleven.'

'So what are you doing dressed in mud, living in a basement? Camping?'

For a moment Lucy looked as if she might hit him, then finally a glimmer of a smile appeared.

'This isn't a joke. My dad was kidnapped. They took him off in a submarine. And my family has disappeared. We haven't found their bodies. I keep hoping –'

There was a long silence. 'I'm sorry,' Winston said finally. 'I had no idea. Do you have any leads on the men who took your dad?'

Lucy shook her head, while behind her Joe, the policeman, scowled.

'Hank – my dad, that is – has one of the biggest sheep farms on the island. Plus he's a lawyer, or he was –' She broke off.

'Other people have also disappeared?' Winston guessed.

'Too right. No one is safe in Paradise any more.'

'Who?'

The girl shrugged. 'You want names? They won't mean anything to you. OK. Matt, the baker. He had four kids. And Mrs Magee, who was a farmer in the south of the island. She just vanished about three weeks ago and no one has seen her since. And Ben Thomas.'

'And the Goldworthys,' Joe cut in. He pointed to the young man standing with his gun by the door. 'This is Paul,' he said, and the man briefly nodded. 'Barry Goldworthy was Paul's cousin. Grew up together like brothers. That close.'

'No one is safe any more,' Lucy repeated. 'Least of all me.'

'So that's why you're hiding here?

'Yeah.' Lucy stopped and looked straight at Winston. 'Weren't we meant to be questioning you?'

'You're afraid,' he prompted her gently.

'They've come looking for me. Back at my house. At Joe's work. And at school. They threatened the headmistress.'

'What do they want?'

Joe said, 'We got that figured. Lucy is a rich girl now. Her dad owned 1,214 acres, the biggest farm on the island –'

Lucy interrupted, 'For a while we couldn't work it out. Pops had no enemies. Nor had Mr Goldworthy. But we were just being plain stupid. It was as obvious as the nose on your face.'

'They want our land,' Joe said heavily. 'They want to take all our land away from us.'

'Plenty of people have sold,' Lucy said.

'They offered us a lot of money. Three or four times what the land is worth,' Joe said.

'Why?' Winston asked.

'Why what?' Lucy replied.

'Why do they want your land so badly? I don't want to be rude, but it's not good for much, is it? Except grazing sheep.'

'We've asked ourselves that a thousand times. You think we're no-brain rednecks? Of course we wondered. Especially when we figured they were killing for land. What's so special about Paradise? It's just a piece of soggy, useless grass.'

Joe was angry. 'Shh, child,' he snapped. 'There's more to Paradise than that.'

'What?' Winston asked, but Joe just shook his head, unwilling or unable to continue. Winston went on, 'It clearly has something. These people are willing to bring down the British government to get their hands on Paradise.'

Lucy walked past the gunmen to the door, looking out for a while at the grey sky and a landscape of rocky turf.

What, Winston wondered, could this grim land possibly have? It wasn't oil. BritOil had explored it carefully. Did the people behind al-Yamani want a base for nuclear weapons – perhaps to threaten America, hold the world to ransom? But then there were islands nearer to the US mainland, if nuclear blackmail was your game.

'You know, it's a funny thing,' Lucy said dreamily. 'I used to hate Paradise. Used to long to go back home to New York. Now I know I belong here. Nothing on earth would make me sell up. I'm going stay here on *my* land, even if they kill me for it in the end.'

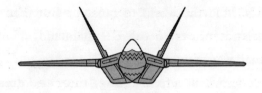

CHAPTER TWENTY-THREE

'This is terrible.' Hugh was pointing to a piece from a newspaper, which he had called up on Winston's laptop. 'How can we stop this?'

The headline blared **RESIGNATIONS TODAY**. The text further down, under a piece headlined **JOHN MINOR – a MAJOR MISTAKE?**, stated that the PM's departure was expected later that day.

Winston glanced at the newspaper and shrugged. They were on an RAF Tristar, flying back home over the Atlantic. He was so shrouded in gloom he could barely bring himself to answer.

'Winston, Minor is innocent! You can't let this happen!'

'Can't I?'

'What are you going to do?'

'Who do you think I am, Superman? I'm just a schoolboy, for heaven's sake?'

Hugh stared at his friend in amazement. 'Just a schoolboy? I'd never thought I'd hear the day when you described yourself as –'

'Yeah, yeah. Shut up a moment. Is a bit of peace too much to ask for?'

Hurt, Hugh relapsed into silence. Winston went back to staring moodily across the bundles and boxes in the middle of the transport plane. He'd come out to Paradise with such high hopes. And those hopes had been dashed by the island's bleak reality. Sure, he'd seen the evil going on in Paradise. But he didn't understand why this mysterious Brigham guy had to have the island. Why had he spent years and millions inventing the character of al-Yamani? Why had he brought down the British government, killing a couple of actors into the bargain?

What could Winston prove? Not a thing! He was just a twelve-year-old who was unusually short for his age. Who would believe his stories of plots and coups? No one, not even GQ.

The day before they left Paradise, Joe, the policeman, had taken the boys to Lucy's farm. It was the same old dreary place: sheep, rain, rocks. Try as he might, Winston could get no insights into why the island and this miserable sheep-shearing station was so desirable.

Never had he felt so powerless.

But it wasn't about power any more. It was about Lucy.

Lucy. The girl's image flickered into life before Winston. Dirty and tangle-haired, eyes burning. Thin hands clutching the heavy pistol. She had the guts to stand up to killers. To live in a dark basement for weeks on end. If she wasn't going to give up, nor was he.

Winston pulled himself up in his seat. He couldn't allow himself the luxury of feeling low. He must fight. Sheer willpower made his brain click into gear. Within seconds it was busy with plans.

'What's eating you?' Hugh asked.

'Just a bit of stomachache,' Winston said. 'Look, I'm sorry I snapped at you, Hugh. I was . . . I was –' He stopped, unsure of how to go on.

'It's OK, Winston,' Hugh said quietly.

The plane had crossed the Channel. Now, as it cut through the quilt of cloud over England, the light changed to a dull grey. England wasn't very different from Paradise. Little wonder the natives of that tiny island felt so British. No wonder Winston wanted to help them so much.

'What are we going to do, Winston? About Minor? And Lucy? You must have some plan?'

Winston turned to his friend gently. 'I think other people have plans for us.'

'What plans?'

'You've forgotten, haven't you?'

'What?'

'The summer holidays are over. We're going back. To Mr Smee.'

'Oh no. *Smee*.' Hugh groaned.

CHAPTER TWENTY-FOUR

'Winston, give us a smile.' A man with three cameras and a vest bulging with lens accessories was leering through the taxi window.

'Over here, matey,' another snapper called. 'Who's your friend?'

'Come on, boy, big it up,' another paparazzo called, sticking his head through the window.

The cab carrying Winston and Hugh back to Duffham Hall had cruised to a standstill. The scrum of cameramen and photographers around the school's wrought-iron gates was so thick, the car was wedged in, like ant stuck in treacle. Looking out through the window, Winston was genuinely bewildered. Why was he being treated like a member of the royal family or a Hollywood superstar?

'What's going on?' he called to a snapper. 'Why is everyone here?'

'You gotta keep up. The PM has resigned. So has Dame Curry and a lot of other politicians. Sir Giles Lushington is standing as the head of a new anti-corruption party.'

Winston let out a bitter laugh.

'It's called True.' The snapper peered in through the window suspiciously. 'What's the joke?'

'Nothing.' Winston choked his laughter back. 'I'm just overtired. So, Sir Giles and True?'

'Yep. The Queen has set the election date. Ten days from tomorrow. But you haven't heard the best bit.'

'It gets better?'

The taxi had found a space in the human jam and began to inch forward.

'Yeah,' the snapper yelled after the retreating car. 'Sir Giles has just named you as his deputy. He's having a photo-call now. At the school gates. That's why we're all here.'

Having found a space, the taxi driver stepped on the gas determinedly and the car moved forward. Photographers jumped out of the way rather than be mown down.

'You can't accept?' Hugh hissed to Winston in an undertone so the taxi driver wouldn't hear. 'Not with what you know about Sir G.'

'Mmm. I'm not sure . . .' The lure of power was tempting and Winston was honest enough to admit it. Visions arose in his head, not so very different from the ones he had at Duffham what seemed like aeons ago.

'He's using you. He wants to hide behind you. To prove he's clean.'

'I know,' Winston replied calmly. 'I'm a sort of human fig leaf to Lushington.'

'Don't give in then. You've gotta turn him down.'

'I'll turn him over instead,' Winston replied.

'Not riddles now. Speak English.'

'I'm going to use *him* for a change.'

'How.'

'Wait and see.'

A smile glimmered around Winston's mouth as the taxi drove through the gates of Duffham Hall. A few months ago he had been promising to be the deputy to another Lushington. But things had changed. This time he was playing for lives, not just a sense of his own importance. This time he wasn't going to be sidelined by a Lushington with more holes in his character than a tea bag.

The majestic sweep of the gravel drive revealed the imposing turrets of the school gleaming beyond. And there was Sir Giles, splendid in a perfect grey suit. He had one arm on the school symbol, a statue of two roaring lions. Three TV cameras were trained on his face as he spoke.

'I want to go BACK TO BASICS. It's time for oldfashioned British values. Unassuming decency, honesty, grit. I want a new, clean Britain. One that is –' Sir Giles caught sight of Winston and stopped mid-flow. He strode over to the taxi and opened the door. 'Where the hell have you been?' he hissed. 'We've all been worried sick about you. Even MI5 hadn't a clue where you'd got to.'

He yanked Winston out of the car by the scruff of his neck.

'The wanderer returns,' Sir Giles said, beaming to the cameras. 'Ladies and gentleman, meet the new Deputy Prime Minister of the new Britain. Ladies and gentleman, meet the face of youth and honesty. Meet Winston Wright.'

A hundred flashbulbs popped – immortalising the moment for tomorrow's front pages Sir Giles Lushington engulfing his chosen deputy, Winston Wright, in a huge hug.

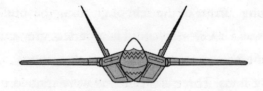

CHAPTER TWENTY-FIVE

THE COMEBACK KID AND THE KID, blared the *Stun*. The papers were full of nicknames for 'the Odd Couple of British Politics', Winston Wright and Sir Giles Lushington.

In the *Crusader* a columnist wrote pompously that Winston added a 'lustre of youthful virtue to the campaign, which, coupled with Sir Giles's undoubted judgement, should give a shattered country new heart'.

Winston read the article in the back seat of the True campaign bus and snorted inwardly. He had been criss-crossing the country with Sir Giles and a team of assistants, shaking hands, kissing babies and making speeches. All for True, a party he didn't believe in. But Winston *did* believe that if he bided his time, he would get his chance.

Sir Giles had been remarkably incurious about Winston's disappearing act. He'd accepted his story that he was tired and went to the seaside 'incognito'. Winston realised this was typical of the man. Sir Giles was too interested in himself to have much left over for other people.

'Can I get you anything, Mr Wright? A cup of tea, some toast, soft drink?' Bob, the assistant, hovered around Winston anxiously, trying to catch his eye. He was in his mid-twenties and had just joined the True campaign team. The assistant was desperate to impress Winston, the likely future Deputy PM of Britain. He really wanted to be an MP himself.

'Thanks, Bob, I'm fine,' Winston said.

'Bob,' Sir Giles's angry roar came from the front seat of the bus. 'The milk in this tea is sour. Is it too much to ask for the basic decencies of life when we're trudging around the country in this depressing fashion?'

'Sorry, sir.' Bob rushed forwards. 'The fridge isn't working properly.'

'Sort yourself out, Bob,' Sir Giles snapped. His face contorted like an angry snake and he threw the tea out of the window on to the bonnet of a passing car. 'You'll never make it at this rate, you bonehead. Work on the basics before you even think about the big time.'

'Yes, Sir Giles,' Bob said humbly.

'I must be the biggest bonehead here then, Sir Giles,' Winston said cheerily. 'I've never cracked making tea. Despite lessons from the best.'

Bob shot Winston a grateful look. But Sir Giles seemed to have recovered his temper.

'Oh, you, Winston.' He leaned out into the corridor, his face wreathed in smiles. 'Of course you're different. Seen the piece in the *Stun*, by the way?'

'Yes, I have,' Winston replied. 'It's some payback, I suppose, for being puked on by that baby in Birmingham.'

It had been an exhausting week. Birmingham yesterday, Manchester today, Sheffield tomorrow. Winston had shaken enough pensioners by the hand, answered enough worries about the oil crisis and crime – not to mention corrupt politicians – to last him a lifetime. Still, the miles on the road in the campaign bus had given him an opportunity to study Sir Giles in close-up. Inside the tough, stinging outer layer, buried in his soggy heart, there was something else – a quality that linked him to the islanders of Paradise. Sir Giles was scared to death.

Winston glanced up from his paper and saw his boss barking into his mobile phone. 'I'm afraid I've had some bad news. Personal matter. Have to meet my accountant.' Sir Giles arrived by Winston's side as the bus took another bend. He was fiddling with his shirt cuffs, a sign that he was flustered. 'Look, I'm awfully sorry. I've had to phone my chauffeur. You better do this wretched meeting on your own.'

When the bus stopped, Sir Giles practically ran to the Jag waiting by the village hall, skilfully eluding the stout matron with a pink rosette who was advancing to meet them.

'Was that Sir Giles?' The matron stared after him, bewildered.

'I'm afraid he won't be able to make the meeting.'

'Never mind. It's you the crowd have come to see, not Sir Giles.'

She turned on Winston with a flirtatious smile. 'But what am I thinking of? I haven't said hello properly.'

Mrs Whipple was determined to kiss Winston and she did, advancing on him like a hungry tigress chasing a deer cub. His feeble protests were no good against her onslaught. One, two, three smackers on each cheek. Sometimes Winston thought he should take more of a back-seat role in politics. Be more of a strategist, a thinker. Anything where he wouldn't have to meet perspiring matrons.

Winston made a brief speech to the packed village hall, setting out his vision. He put things straight – and explained that harsh measures were needed to prevent the world energy shortage becoming a calamity. Then he took questions. There were a few from journalists, a few from the crowd. A girl about Winston's age put up her hand.

'Will kids have the vote? I mean, it's not really fair if we don't. You get to be in the government and decide lots of things. We don't have a say on anything.'

Winston had foreseen this question. It was a tricky one. Still, kids couldn't make more of a hash of things than adults had. 'It's not something *I* can decide,' he said. 'Perhaps it should be put to the vote.'

'I've got another question,' the girl went on determinedly.

'Go for it.'

'Sir Giles Lushington is a bit of a greaseball. How do you know that he won't do the dirty on you once you've got him elected?'

Winston laughed and the outraged murmurs at the girl's cheek settled.

'Good question. Though not one Sir Giles would like. How can you trust anyone in politics? Or indeed life? My answer is that Sir Giles was foolish, once. But

I believe in second chances.' He turned his eyes on the girl. 'Do you?'

The girl flushed hotly. 'Yeah. I s'pose . . . I mean, they let me back in school after I was expelled for turning on the fire alarm during assembly.'

Winston's mobile went off just as he left the stage to enthusiastic cheering. He sidestepped the matron, who looked as if she was gearing up for another of her hugs, and took the call. It was Hugh.

'I've had some amazing news. Amazing. You've got to come to Duffham. Right now,' Hugh was shouting into the phone. 'Drop everything and come to Duffham.'

'What? Why?'

'I can't tell you over the phone. It's not safe.' There was a small explosion in the background. 'Crikey!' Hugh dropped the phone.

'Hugh? Are you all right?'

'Yeah. Yeah. Of course. I'm fine.' Hugh was back on the line. 'You've got to see this, Winston. It's amazing.'

Winston hung up and hurried back to the campaign bus, taking out his personal organiser on the way and connecting with GQ's miniature camera. He had palmed this speck-sized piece of spyware on to Sir Giles's jacket before he went to meet his 'accountant'.

There was Sir Giles, shaking a very fat hand. The

camera had a restricted view, so he caught only a glimpse of face – a chubby one wearing dark glasses. As he froze the frame, Winston was willing to swear it was the man he had seen in the boxing club. The sound on the camera bug had malfunctioned, so he wasn't able to hear what they were talking about. In fact he was lucky that Brigham Hope's men hadn't spotted the bug in the first place. Or maybe Brigham had left his minders at home. From what he could see on the camera, there were no bodyguards around. Just one very fat man, barely visible under his enormous tinted specs, sitting opposite Sir Giles in a village tea shop.

Winston cursed GQ's fancy device. The fancier the gadget, the more often it broke down. The man slid a fat brown paper envelope across the table towards Sir Giles. The head of True opened the packet and looked inside. Because of the angle of the camera Winston couldn't see what he was looking at. The camera went all wobbly, as if Sir Giles had become agitated. The fat hand took the sheaf of papers and put them back in the envelope. He waved the envelope about as though taunting Sir Giles with it. Sir Giles waved his hands in an agitated manner.

Winston didn't know what was in the envelope.

But he could make a very good guess at what it all meant.

His mind went back to the scandal at the Alka Salsa nightclub, when Sir Giles was snapped in a grass skirt.

Blackmail.

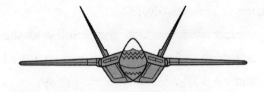

CHAPTER TWENTY-SIX

'Winston, my boy, how twemendously we have missed you. Life at Duffham hasn't been the same since you deserted us for gweater things.'

Roger Smee, Duffham's headmaster, was in the middle of a group of excited boys, including Winston's friend Toby Smith. Smee was bustling about, trying to get noticed by the cameramen who had arrived for the election photo-call. When he spotted his former pupil he swooped down on him.

'Term's only been going a week and a half,' Winston pointed out mildly.

'Still, you've left quite a hole. We weally have been pining for you.' Smee swivelled round and gave the TV cameras a beaming smile. 'This young man turned our school upside down,' he announced to the press. 'In fact we're planning a new Winston Wight scholarship memowial fund.'

'A memorial fund? I'm not dead yet,' Winston protested.

'No, no. You misunderstand me. We are intending to honour one of the most wemarkable boys we've ever –'

Toby Smith started giggling.

'I hope you've not got my obituary prepared, headmaster. I know I got on your nerves, but surely you don't want me in a box?'

Toby's giggles were infectious. Soon all the boys were laughing. Even when Smee turned his steely glare on them they refused to stop. After all, what was a mere head teacher compared to Winston?

'You will have your little joke, won't you, Winston? I don't have favouwites, as you know, but you were weally vewy special to me.'

'A special pain in neck.' Winston smiled blandly at Smee. 'By the way, headmaster, how are your religious and moral education sessions going?'

The headmaster blanched.

'The headmaster runs special classes for hand-picked pupils. On things like leadership skills, manners and, er, toilet maintenance,' Winston told the press with a grin. 'Toby here keeps me up to date with their progress, don't you?'

'Yes, I do,' said Toby, and a dozen cameras swivelled round to focus on him. 'We talk on the phone the whole time. In fact, Winston, you said you'd pop back for one of Mr Smee's sessions soon.'

'Always flattered to have the wemarkable Winston with us,' Smee said weakly.

Winston smiled pleasantly at the headmaster, who was trying hard to control his irritation. It was time to find Hugh. He slipped away from his bodyguards and went into the school. Walking by the chemistry lab, he was stopped in his tracks by a peculiar smell. It was rich and sweet, but slightly bitter. It made his nose twitch. Stewing almonds perhaps or burnt vanilla. It wasn't pleasant – but not exactly unpleasant either.

There was Hugh hunched over, watching intently as purple liquid bubbled in test tubes. The curtains of the lab were drawn and things were cooking in several large burners. Hugh looked as if he hadn't slept for days. Winston spotted his razor and toothbrush by the tubes. Had he been bedding down in the lab? There were bags under his eyes, his hair stood up in greasy spikes and he had his t-shirt on inside out.

'Winston, thanks for coming. Look, you won't

believe what happens when you bleach the stuff with high-octane propane. It's got unbelievable calorifc value.'

'Hugh, what are you doing with all these test tubes? You haven't gone all brainy on me?'

Hugh beamed. 'It's unbelievably exciting. I've never seen such a dramatic reaction.'

'What on earth are you talking about?'

Hugh glanced at Winston briefly. 'What on Paradise, more like!'

'Stop being mysterious. What is this stuff?' Winston gestured to the bubbling liquid. 'What's going on?'

Hugh gazed blearily at his friend. 'Use your eye, Winston. Just look at it.'

He pointed at the packets on the table. Winston recognised the samples his friend had collected on Paradise.

'Your old rocks. So what?'

When Hugh began to laugh, there was an edge of hysteria to the sound. So unlike solid, dependable Hugh. 'It's Paradise rock. Paradise really rocks. It's a supersonic wonder-fuel.'

'Wonder-fuel,' Winston said slowly, his brain refusing to work.

'It's amazing, this muck. These crystals can just burn and burn.'

'What? But I thought your rocks were just a pile of old rubble.'

'Rubble that's worth a fortune.'

Winston stared at the burner. It sounded impossible. No, not impossible, improbable.

'If you don't believe me, look at this.' Hugh put a tiny speck of rock near the Bunsen burner, doused it with liquid and lit it.

The crystal started to behave in the most extra-ordinary way. It began to fizz and glow a most un-earthly purple. It lit even the furthest corners of the room with an extra-planetary luminance. Whoosh. In a second the whole countertop was roaring with flames.

'Hell,' shrieked Hugh. 'That's the biggest reaction I've seen. He ran and got a glass of water, which he tossed on the flames. But the speck of rock seemed to just get a kick from the water. It burned with extra dazzling radiance.

At this rate they could burn down the school in half an hour.

'What shall we do?' screamed Hugh.

'Get the fire blanket,' Winston suggested.

Hugh dived for the blanket and threw it over the flames.

A mobile began to ring. One of the annoyingly loud

novelty ringtones Hugh had recorded for Winston. A deep version of 'Swing Low, Sweet Chariot'.

'Sorry. Got to get this,' Winston yelled as Hugh held the blanket over the countertop. 'Hello,' he snapped into the phone. 'What? Yes, I'm coming. Listen, I'm OK. I'll be back in a minute.' Winston hung up. 'That was Bob, one of my minders. The staff panic if I'm out of their sight for two minutes,' he explained awkwardly to Hugh, who was sweating, glowing purple in the strange light. He looked like some strange boiled vegetable.

'That's OK,' said Hugh. When he took away his hand, he saw that a red burn had spread over it. 'Crikey. Now I know how you felt when you burnt you hand in that shed.'

The flames were dying down. The purple glow of Paradise rock turned pink. Then a moment later the glow faded and it was just a speck of crystalline rock on the counter of a school chemistry lab.

Winston's legs had turned to water. He sat down on one of the metal lab chairs with a thump. For once he simply couldn't think of anything clever to say.

'What is Paradise rock?'

'I don't really know,' Hugh confessed. 'It's magic stuff, though, isn't it?' Hugh took one of the hard lumps in his fingers. The bittersweet smell in the lab was now so strong it was almost impossible to breathe. 'Absolutely amazing.'

'It's awesome. It could solve the world energy crisis. In one stroke . . . If we could use it as fuel.'

'And I'll show you how.'

Hugh put a tiny fragment of the rock in a gizmo sitting on the top of the desk that looked like an old car battery with wires coming out of it.

'This battery is completely dead. I got it out of Smee's car, by the way. With me so far?'

'Of course. Get on with it.'

'Well, I've put some Paradise rock in it. Now I've added some of this liquid. Come on.'

Winston followed his bodyguard down the hall towards the basement of the school. The generating room was past the kitchen in the depths of the cellars. It was strictly out of bounds. As they tiptoed along, Winston thought about the impact of Hugh's find. If this was true, it would explain why Brigham Hope wanted Paradise Island.

Paradise was full of this amazing rock. That meant the owner of Paradise would be rich. Amazingly rich. But more than rich, they would be powerful. The person who controlled Paradise would have the presidents and prime ministers of the world eating out of his hands – like a bunch of tame sheep.

Winston and Hugh sneaked past cook and down some steep cobwebby steps. The generator was in the corner of the cellar. It was an old-fashioned machine controlled by a big lever. A meter by the side showed how much electricity the school was consuming. Hugh pulled the lever down, the electricity metre cut out and the school came to a standstill. Lights, computers, fridges, cookers, everything went bang.

A TV crew that had plugged into the school energy source – to interview the headmaster on his role in creating the Winston phenomenon – found their lights and machines stopped dead. Smee was cut off mid-sentence.

Down in the basement, with the help of a torch, Hugh plugged the doctored car battery into the school generator. The lights came back on. 'I'll leave the Paradise rock in the generator. Remember the tiny bit of the gloop I put in is now the only source of electricity across the school,' Hugh explained proudly. 'Come on, let's go upstairs and have a look.'

The two boys trooped up the stairs again. Winston didn't need to see the evidence of the rock's miracle power. He could *hear* it, in the whirr of the blender as cook devised that day's torture for the pupils of Duff-ham Hall. The TV was on somewhere and an electric piano was playing. It was all so normal. As they walked down the corridor, Winston felt increasingly thunderstruck.

This was revolutionary. Paradise rock would rock England. It would change the entire world.

And the person who had discovered this all was . . . Well, certainly not Winston, not the boy genius. It was Hugh, his bodyguard, who had found the solution to the mystery while Winston flailed in the dark. Hugh deserved a bit of praise.

'Um, Hugh, a brilliant find, by the way. Really amazing. You're turning into Duffham's Einstein. How did you do it?'

Hugh reddened.

'Come on,' Winston prompted.

'It was nothing really.'

'Don't be coy.'

'Actually it was an accident,' Hugh admitted reluctantly.

'An accident?'

'Um, well, I was having a bit of a, em . . . well, you see, the fact of the matter is I had a bit of a fire.'

'Hugh! Not your revolting cigars again?'

'Er, yes, as a matter of fact.'

'This isn't the time for a lecture on mortality statistics. What happened?'

'I was smoking the cigar when suddenly I heard a knock on the door. I had to hide it, of course, so I put it out quickly and stuffed it in my desk drawer. 'Actually it wasn't one of the teachers or anything. It was just Toby. Toby Smith. He was asking about you, as a matter of fact . . .

'After he'd gone I smelt the weirdest smell. It was sort of bitter and sweet. I know you think my cigars are smelly, but this was much stronger. Almost delicious but a bit disgusting at the same time.

'I opened my drawer and found the cigar had sort of burnt out. But the strange thing was the rocks. There's something in the combination of nicotine and fire that ignites them. There was this bluish-purple light coming out of the drawer. It was fizzing and burning purple. Like an alien had landed in there. I couldn't believe it. The rock went on glowing for hours . . . so I thought I'd take it to the chemistry lab . . . and, well, you've seen the rest.'

'You've won me over, Hugh. I'm beginning to see the benefits of cigars,' Winston said as they walked out of the school's front door and on to the drive. 'The world has a lot to thank them for.'

As soon as they emerged, people descended on Winston like a hive on a queen bee. In an instant he was in the centre of a scrum of minders, kids, reporters and the inevitable Roger Smee. This wasn't the time for chit-chat. Winston moved ruthlessly through the throng, mowing them down as he said hurried goodbyes.

Hugh shouted, 'What happens now? Is it going to be all right?' His plea was swallowed up by the din around his friend. Winston looked so small alongside his burly bodyguards. Too young to stop this horrible plot. As he trudged back to school, Hugh was seized by a feeling of dread.

CHAPTER TWENTY-SEVEN

'It's all over, Sir Giles.'

'Wonderful, isn't it? The election's over and the exit polls show we've won the biggest landslide ever.'

'Let's hope it doesn't bury us,' Winston muttered. 'But I'm not talking about the election. This is more serious – I know everything about the plot, about Brigham Hope and Paradise Island.'

Sir Giles looked at Winston and blinked several times, as if he couldn't quite *understand* what he was saying.

'I know how you got rid of John Minor and Stella Curry and all the other politicians. I know all about the sting . . .'

The future Prime Minister drew himself up very tall. 'What are you talking about? You've always had an imagination. This time I'm afraid you're letting it run away with you –'

Winston carried on, speaking over Sir Giles's protests. 'I even know the details. How you set up the video trap. How you got two unemployed actors to play Abacus and al-Yamani. How Brigham Hope planned and funded it all . . .

'Who killed the actors, by the way? Was it you?'

'No,' Sir Giles burst out indignantly. 'That was – I don't know what you're talking about.'

'Brigham Hope,' Winston said. 'I thought so. Didn't think you really had murder in your blood.'

Sir Giles was still protesting. Winston turned the searchlight of his eyes on him and the minister sputtered to a halt.

'I know everything, Sir Giles. And you know what? . . . I don't care.'

'You don't care!' This statement left Sir Giles thunderstruck. He looked at Winston foolishly. 'What! I mean –'

The man was shrinking before Winston's eyes.

'I don't care,' Winston said firmly. 'It's all in the past now. History can sort it out. What I *do* care about is Paradise Island.'

'That blasted place. I hear you can't throw a stone

on Paradise Island without hitting a sheep on the head. Or, what's worse, a peasant.'

Winston's winced at the minister's unpleasant talk.

'I don't like that sort of snobbery. Who owns Paradise now?'

'Why does everyone get so worked up about it? It's a sheep-infested hole.'

'It has something we all want.'

Sir Giles laughed nastily. 'Don't tell me. Oil. Paradise is the new Saudi Arabia.'

Winston didn't crack a smile. 'Something better.'

The older man wasn't listening. 'It can't be oil. BritOil checked the place out years ago. I read the report when Brigham started sniffing round the place.'

Winston got up and walked to the window. The sun was setting on the Houses of Parliament. People had finished marking their voting forms with an X earlier that day. The booths had shut up shop. And across the country volunteers were working through the night to count the ballot papers – votes, which if the polls were to be believed, would make the rotten man behind him the country's next PM. Winston turned from the window. 'No, Sir Giles. Not oil. Paradise Island has something infinitely more powerful. A rock. A rock that is a unique and miraculous energy source.'

Sir Giles slumped down in his armchair and put his head in his hands. 'It sounds like science fiction,' he muttered.

'It's all right.' Winston said. 'Your bacon can be saved as long as you haven't given Paradise to Brigham.'

The Prime Minster-elect looked up. He had gone pale.

'I have.'

'You *idiot*,' Winston blurted out. 'Did you sign the papers with a lawyer and witnesses present?'

'Yesterday,' Sir Giles said, nodding miserably. 'I had to. He wanted it.'

'*He wanted it*? And if I want the moon?'

'He nagged and nagged at me. There was nothing I could do.'

The most powerful man in Britain made a pathetic sight as he cowered in his gilt armchair. Winston looked down on him, contempt written on his face.

'Do you know what you've done?'

The Prime Minister-elect didn't reply.

'Before I left Paradise, I gave a girl called Lucy Carter a camera and a computer. This is the message I received from her twenty minutes ago.'

On the computer's screen was a download taken from the other side of the world. Through dust and smoke a picture of giant diggers and earthmovers filled the screen. Ant-like men marched here and there in thick lines. They were loading great sacks on to lorries. It was a scene of frenzied activity. The camera pulled out and you could see the character-istic squelchy green fields of Paradise. The time code on the top of the camera read '6.30 a.m., 15 September' in luminous green script.

'So? Someone doing a bit of digging.' Sir Giles made an attempt to shrug off the pictures.

'Don't worry. It gets worse.'

The time code spooled forward: 7.30 a.m. The camera was wobbling all over the place, as if the person carrying it was running. A bag dumped on the street, with underwear, jewellery and a child's yellow plastic Bob the Builder truck spilling out. Then the camera jerked upwards, a woman wailing out, a toddler screaming. Behind them a man in a mask pointing a gun. The camera swung around: the street was full of people, bags, cars, men with guns. Gunshots sounded. Some sheep had wandered into the street.

Then the screen went black.

'What does it mean?' Sir Giles clutched at his head, pulling at his greased-back hair. 'What on earth *can* it mean?'

'You know what it means. But I'll spell it out for you if you insist,' Winston snapped. 'That's the capital of Paradise, Port Eve. Men with guns are evicting people from their homes. I should think that Brigham Hope has claimed ownership of Paradise. After all, you signed it over to him.'

'My God, this is ghastly. I had no idea. I thought he wanted the damn place as a retreat. His own private island. You know Brigham is a recluse.'

'A recluse?' asked Winston.

'He hardly every goes out. When he does he wears dark glasses. He hates people.'

'And you signed over the people of Paradise to that man. I should think these scenes will be on the news within the hour. What are you going to do about it?'

CHAPTER TWENTY-EIGHT

Thump! General Percy Skower banged the table with an angry fist. 'This cannot be allowed to continue,' he roared. 'This means war.'

The joint chiefs of staff were ranged around a huge table which gleamed with varnish. Their fronts gleamed too, with glittering medals and jangling decorations. Percy, the head of the army, had scarcely a centimetre of blue tunic free from metal. He was pulling away from his nearest competitor, the head of the air force, in the final furlong of the great medal race.

At the head of the table Sir Giles, his face raw and sweaty, looked very bedraggled by contrast. 'What do you suggest, Percy?' he muttered.

'Send in the SAS, with two regiments to back 'em up. They can be there in under a day.'

Sir Giles looked round the table, a haunted man. 'Anyone else have any suggestions?'

There was silence from the generals. Then GQ, Winston's old friend from MI5, piped up. 'We've just had a communication handed to us. It is from the Rooters News Agency. Shall I?'

'Go ahead.' Sir Giles shrugged. His speech was coming out slightly slurred. Winston, who was sitting next to him, could smell the whisky on his breath.

'A man called Brigham Hope sent it to Rooters five minutes ago. It's going out to the world about now.' The man from MI5 glanced at his watch. 'No one in my team has heard of this Brigham Hope. Ring any bells with the rest of you?'

Sir Giles let out another faint groan, which he quickly supressed. In the silence that followed GQ read out the message:

MY NAME IS BRIGHAM HOPE. I AM THE NEW OWNER OF PARADISE ISLAND. THE ISLAND WAS SIGNED OVER TO ME BY THE BRITISH PM, SIR GILES LUSHINGTON, IN THE PRESENCE OF TWO LAWYERS AND TWO INDEPENDENT WITNESSES.

I AM EVICTING THE RESIDENTS OF PARADISE BECAUSE THE ISLAND IS NOW MINE. THEIR HOMES WILL BE TAKEN BY MY OWN MEN, WHO ARE NEEDED TO WORK THE FABULOUS NEW MINES OF PARADISE.

THE GLITTERING MINES CONTAIN A MIRACLE ROCK, WHICH I HAVE NAMED HOPEITE.

HOPEITE. REMEMBER THAT NAME, LADIES AND GENTLEMEN, FOR IT WILL CHANGE THE WORLD.

HOPEITE WILL GIVE THE WORLD HOPE. IT WILL POWER THE SCHOOLS, THE FACTORIES AND THE CITIES OF TOMORROW. IT WILL CONQUER SPACE. AT A SINGLE STROKE IT WILL END QUEUES AND SHORTAGES.

IMAGINE A ROCK HOLDING MORE POWER THAN NUCLEUR FUEL, BUT WITHOUT ANY OF THE ATTENDANT DANGERS. PARADISE IS TEEMING WITH THIS MIRACLE FUEL. AND I CONTROL IT ALL.

BE WARNED. NO ONE WILL BE ABLE

TO TAKE PARADISE FROM ME BY FORCE. MY MINES ARE BOOBY-TRAPPED AND WILL BE BLOWN UP IN THE EVENT OF ANY ATTACK ON ME OR MY INTERESTS. THE EXPLOSION WOULD BE ON A NUCLEAR SCALE AND THE FABULOUS ROCK FIELDS OF PARADISE WOULD BE LOST TO THE WORLD FOREVER.

I WILL CONTACT THE WORLD WITH MY DEMANDS IN MY OWN TIME.

GQ came to the end of the message. The generals and politicians stared at him dumbfounded. Then, as one, they all turned and stared at Sir Giles.

'I-I-I –' the PM stuttered.

The red hotline from the President of the USA, which was always kept open for world emergencies, began to ring. The PM picked it up and a deep Southern twang resounded throughout the room. The American President was steaming, boiling mad. 'Lushington, what the hell is going on?' President Houston yelled. 'Who is Brigham Hope? Why'd you give this feller Paradise Island? How the heck are we going to get a slice of this miracle gunk?'

Sir Giles stuttered. He didn't need to look at the expressions on the faces of the generals. He got up and sidled to the door. When the going gets rough, Sir Giles usually arranged a meeting with his best friend: The bottle. 'Fact of the matter is I have to go. Urgent, um, appointment,' he muttered. 'Er, be back in a minute.'

'Spineless. No backbone. Gutless.' The comments sprang up around the table, hissing from medal to medal.

Someone had to take control.

'Percy,' Winston said, 'I want you to prepare the battle plans. We need to be ready to go by 4 p.m. I want two full regiments and an SAS vanguard in battle readiness.'

'But on whose authority?' General Skower asked, bewildered.

'On mine. The Deputy Prime Minister of Britain. And on that of Sir Giles Lushington, the PM,' Winston said firmly.

'But you're just a –' General Skower began before Winston squelched him with a look.

Winston turned to Air Admiral Richard Flitwick. 'Richard, have a squadron of parachutists ready. You can land and await orders on Penguin Rock, just two miles from Paradise Island.

'But what about the booby-trapped mines. And the guy may have surface-to-air missiles,' Flitwick protested. 'I'd be sending my men into a death trap.'

'Don't you worry about that,' Winston said calmly. He stood up and turned to the intelligence chief. 'GQ, could you come with me. I need a word.'

GQ rose instantly.

If there was one person in the room who realised that Winston wasn't in the government as window-dressing it was GQ.

CHAPTER TWENTY-NINE

'You've come to shee me. My only true friend in the whole wide, wide world. It ish a big world, ishn't it?'

With irritation, Winston saw that Sir Giles had reached the maudlin stage of drunkenness that was so common with him. Self-pity seeped from every whisky-soaked pore in his body.

'Je ne regrette rien. Whatever must be must be. The future is ours, you see. Que sera sera,' the PM began to warble, mixing up his favourite tunes.

'Don't talk rubbish. I am not your only friend. There's Lady Lushington. And your son, Jago. They care for you deeply.'

The PM stopped singing. If you could call it singing.

'Lady Lush, shee only caresh for fancy clothes and jewels and nice houses. Shees materialishtic. And my shon, Jago. Bit of a fool. Ushelesh.' The PM filled up his beaker with whisky, unmixed with water, Winston noted.

'Like father, like son then,' Winston couldn't resist saying. Without the PM noticing, he took the beaker and hid it behind a pile of books.

For a moment the suspicion that his deputy was laughing at him glimmered in Sir Giles's eyes. Then the light of mammalian intelligence went out. 'What am I going to do?' he wailed. The tears gushed forth. 'People are going to find out. I'm finisshed. Theresh nothing I can do.'

'There is one thing you can do. There is one thing you can do that will rescue your dignity.'

'There ish?' Wild hope gleamed in the PM's eyes 'What ish it?'

'Resign.'

'But I don't want to reshign. I want to be prime minishter. It's what I've always wanted. Since I was a boy.'

'Lushington, you go now or you will be kicked out.'

The PM looked pleadingly at Winston. He had spilled whisky on his white shirt front. His nose had reddened and swelled up. 'Pleashe. Pleashe let me be PM.'

'No.'

'Pleashe.'

'No. Absolutely not.'

'All right,' he said miserably. 'Tell me what to do.'

'The first thing to do is to sort you out. Clean shirt, I think. Comb your hair. Come on.'

The PM staggered up and, supported by his deputy, tottered to the toilet that led off the study. There Winston splashed water on his face and advised him on his change of clothes. Then he took him downstairs to the pillared room where the PM entertained foreign heads of state.

The BBC were waiting there, summoned by Winston. The glorious room, complete with Persian carpets, crystal chandeliers and large pillars, was blazing with hot TV lights. Cameramen fiddled with their equipment. The TV producer was buzzing around like a hornet.

Winston had, of course, prepared a statement for Sir Giles to read. He considered there was less chance of cock-up that way.

The PM sat down at the desk and looked at the short, typewritten paragraphs. Then woodenly he began, reciting the text as if he was reading out a list of numbers:

'I, Shir Gishes Lushington, have always wished to serve my country. Jush a few days ago I was elected PM by a huge majority of voters.

'But sadly I have found my new government in crisis. The situation in Paradise threatens the stability of the country. I find that I am not fit to lead you as I would wish. Sadly I am not as well in health as I would want to be.

'Therefore I must resign my position as Prime Minister . . . hic. My doctors have advised me to spend more time with my family – something I have always found hard to do, because serving my country has come first –'

Sir Giles broke off, a rosy alcoholic flush spreading over his face.

'But I don't want to spend more time with my family,' he whined. 'You've met 'em, haven't you? I want to be –'

'Cut!' Winston barged in front of the cameras. 'You can't use that one,' he said firmly to the producer. 'Come on, give me the tape.'

The producer was protesting about his journalistic freedom when Winston removed the tape from the camera.

'Now, if a word of this gets to the papers,' he said

to the camera crew, 'I will personally see to it that you never, ever get access to government stories again. I don't believe in kicking a man when he is down. But if you're good, if you do the kind thing, you'll be rewarded.'

'Agreed, Winston – I mean, Deputy PM,' the producer replied. 'But I want exclusive stories.'

'You'll have your exclusives,' Winston said impatiently.

Meanwhile the PM had slumped down on the desk. Winston went over to him and, putting his arm around him, forced him upright. He somehow got a reviving glass of cold water down his throat. Then Sir Giles went through his resignation speech again. This time without a hitch.

At the final words, 'I name my deputy, Winston Wright, as Prime Minister, until full elections are held,' Sir Giles broke off from the script again. 'You'll like Winston,' he said, looking at the TV camera for the first time. 'He'll sort you out. Goodness knows, he tried to sort me out.'

CHAPTER THIRTY

The new Prime Minister of Britain was about to make his first speech to Parliament. Before him were ranks of subdued MPs. Across the country people were glued to their televisions. The speech was due to run on all main networks. Winston the boy in a hurry had achieved far more than he had ever seriously imagined. A PM at age twelve and a bit. It was almost bizarre.

But the times were bizarre. People were scared of the future and didn't know who to trust. They were turning to unlikely saviours. A former movie stuntman was the President of the USA and a former dog-trainer the President of France.

So he'd made it. Achieved the power he always craved. But now that he was here in front of all these expectant faces, he didn't find it quite as exciting as he'd imagined. What was making his mouth dry and hands sticky wasn't power. It was responsibility.

While Paradise was savaged by Brigham Hope's army, Britain was tipping into anarchy. There had been riots in Brighton and looting in Edinburgh. A mob had gathered to demonstrate in London, but then, undecided what they were protesting about, had dispersed. The power crisis was worse than ever. Across the country factories and schools, offices and cinemas ground to a halt. Even hospitals had to cancel non-urgent operations and send some of their patients back home.

All his life Winston had suffered from the feeling that he was running on fifty per cent of his full capacity. That had changed. He was fully charged now. Planning the invasion with the generals, fielding questions from the press, writing his speech, dealing with the power crisis and keeping in touch with Lucy in Paradise.

In fact he was seriously worried about Lucy. The emails from her had suddenly stopped. And she wasn't on the lists of boat people leaving Paradise that the Foreign Office had circulated. Where was she? Had she drowned? Or had Brigham's men got her?

Winston coughed – and like a many-headed beast cowed by the authority of its trainer – the MPs fell silent. His voice, when he spoke, would have carried into every corner of the chamber even without a microphone:

'I know I have the body of a weak and vertically challenged boy. But I have the heart and stomach of a Prime Minister, and of a Prime Minister of Great Britain too. And I think foul scorn that any man should dare invade the borders of my realm, however far away those borders are drawn.

Brigham Hope, a man who hides behind a cloak of mystery, has had the cheek to invade a country that is under our protection. I promise every man, woman and child in Paradise that he will not take their island away from them. Today he faces the full might of Great Britain.

We will not let injustice triumph. We will fight them. With words, with the law or with whatever weapon we chose . . . And we will win. Because right is on our side.'

His speech had taken all of fifty-five seconds. Winston began to walk to the door – he'd said all he needed to. But a storm broke out in the house.

'When are you going to hold elections?' someone shouted.

'What about the energy crisis?'

'You can't beat Brigham's bomb,' came a desperate wail.

Winston stopped. 'I am not just your Prime Minister, I am also your commander-in-chief,' he told them. 'And as your commander-in-chief I ask you to trust me. Trust me for twenty-four hours. That's all I ask you to do.' The Prime Minister smiled. 'I really don't see that you have any choice.'

A helicopter was ready on the launch pad on top of the Ministry of Defence. A bodyguard was waiting for him by the helicopter, his hair standing straight up in the wind from the rotor blades. It made him look even taller than usual.

'I couldn't believe it when Smee let me off school, what with my A levels coming up.' Hugh was buzzing with excitement. 'Trust you to quote Queen Elizabeth I in your speech. You know what, Winston, I don't think you want to be PM. You want to be king!'

Winston grinned and slapped Hugh on the back.

'Where we going?

'I see you're not wearing your Bermuda shorts this time.'

'Paradise?'

The new PM nodded.

CHAPTER THIRTY-ONE

The windswept rock was a scene of well-drilled activity. Lines of SAS men with blackened faces and grubby fatigues were going through their manoeuvres. Hugh didn't look out of place in their midst. If anything, he was taller than the average commando.

The task force's preparations were deadly secret. The men were forbidden to turn on their radios or even talk above a whisper. GQ had spread a high-frequency sonic net over the tiny rock which would hopefully shield their activity from Brigham's men. The foggy weather helped too.

Over the rim of the horizon the sun was slowly sinking into the sea. It was a sight of rare beauty, spilling scarlet, gold and purple rays into the blackish water, refracting beams through the dense clouds. For a moment Winston let his papers slip out of his hand and gave himself over to enjoying the sunset. He had finally heard from Lucy. His plans were ready.

'Hrrmph.' He heard a coughing at his side. It was General Percy Skower.

'PM, we've just had another message from Brigham Hope. It was sent to Rooters again.'

Winston took the typescript and read:

I AM SICK OF LIFE ON EARTH. THIS PLANET IS A MESS. IT IS DIRTY, AND OVERCROWDED WITH REVOLTING PEOPLE. THE AIR IS POISONED WITH LEAD AND CARBON DIOXIDE. THE TREES ARE STUNTED. THE VERY FISH IN THE SEA ARE DYING BECAUSE OF NOXIOUS CHEMICALS.

EVEN IN THE WILDS OF NEVADA OR THE GOBI DESERT OR ALASKA, EVEN ON THE BEAUTIFUL SLOPES OF MOUNT EVEREST, IT IS IMPOSSIBLE TO GET AWAY ENTIRELY FROM HUMAN POLLUTION. YOU FIND THINGS. NASTY THINGS. EMPTY CRISP PACKETS OR SMELLY FAST-

FOOD CARTONS. COKE CANS OR WADS OF USED CHEWING GUM.

MY SOUL SHUDDERS AT THE INTRUSION.

AND OF COURSE THERE IS ALWAYS, JUST ALWAYS, THE RISK CAUSED BY THE WORST POLLUTANT OF ALL: PEOPLE.

WHAT IS A SENSITIVE PERSON TO DO? HOW TO GET AWAY FROM THIS HUMAN RUBBISH?

AFTER MUCH AGONISING, I HAVE COME TO THE ONLY CONCLUSION POSSIBLE.

I MUST HAVE THE MOON.

I WILL MAKE IT MY HOME. IT WILL BE A PLACE OF PEACE AND LIGHT – FAR AWAY FROM THE MENACE OF ANYONE DROPPING IN TO SEE ME.

I WILL KEEP THE MOON CLEAN AND BEAUTIFUL, FREE FROM DRIVE-IN HAMBURGER JOINTS AND CHAIN STORES. IT WILL ALWAYS SHINE ON THE WORLD – AND YOU CAN SLEEP IN YOUR BEDS AT NIGHT, SAFE IN THE

KNOWLEDGE THAT NO ONE IS
DESPOILING ITS TIMELESS SERENITY
WITH ASTROTURF AND MINI GOLF
COURSES.

IN RETURN FOR THE MOON I,
BRIGHAM HOPE, WILL SUPPLY YOU
WITH AS MUCH ENERGY AS I DECIDE
THAT YOU NEED. I NEED HARDLY ADD
THAT YOU WILL PAY MY PRICE. I WILL
GIVE YOU TILL MIDNIGHT TONIGHT –
GREENWICH MEAN TIME – TO AGREE
TO MY DEMANDS.

Across the planet printing presses whirred. Online
news agencies whizzed. TV stations buzzed.

'EARTH 0, MOON 1,' headlined the *Times of
India*. 'MY OWN STAIRWAY TO HEAVEN,'
proclaimed the *Washington Post*.

'OUR PLANET DOESN'T SUCK,' whinged the
tabloid *Stun*.

On Penguin Rock Winston let his newspaper drop
from his hand, a bemused smile on his face. Given the
current race between China and America to colonise
space, he felt a sneaking sympathy for Brigham's
demands. Winston didn't want to go to drive-in

movies on the moon either. The man was a maniac. But an interesting one.

General Skower was still standing in front of him. 'We're one hundred per cent ready, PM,' the general said quietly. 'Should I give the order to go?'

Winston glanced at the sun. It had disappeared into the Atlantic, draining the light out of the world. 'OK.' He nodded.

CHAPTER THIRTY-TWO

Winston had consulted nobody about this plan – not France and Germany, not even the President of the USA, traditionally Britain's closest ally. If it failed there would just be one head on the chopping block. His.

At 11 p.m., GMT sixty hand-picked SAS commandos trooped on to the A1 Stealth flyers. These were a recently designed prototype, so secret that nobody outside their crews and a handful of top people knew about them. Supersonic, lightweight, a giant flying wing, they could go for over 11,500 miles without refuelling and were totally – not virtually – undetectable to enemy radar. They could also land on almost any terrain.

Stealth flyers were Winston's secret weapon. He

watched with a touch of regret as two of them lifted off for Paradise. They flew through the thick clouds like giant albatrosses. His generals had forbidden Winston to accompany the SAS commandos. He was needed at HQ.

The two jets landed with a pneumatic hiss in a grassy bog near Lucy's father's farm. The commandos slithered out of the planes as silently as eels out of a tin can, their feet sinking in the marsh. Hugh, his face blackened and wearing miner's gear, accompanied the vanguard. The men fanned out and crept towards the complex. A fifteen-foot barbed-wire fence, strung with top-of-the-range heat and motion sensors, guarded the mine. The perimeter was patrolled every fifteen minutes.

At 11.35 p.m. GMT two men put 'the Mole', a lightweight tunnelling machine, in place. Within minutes a tunnel deep under the fence had been excavated. Scrambling as fast as they could, the men went through in pairs. The whole operation took eight and a half minutes. There was always the danger that one of Brigham's guards would spot the tunnel. Or even fall into it. But it was a danger they would have to live with.

The commandos split up. A third of the men went to the mouth of the mine to tackle the guards there. Another third peeled off to the barracks. And the final third, including Hugh, made for a run-down shack that stood close to the mouth of the mine. It had a rusty corrugated-tin roof and battered wooden sides. It looked as if it had been abandoned for years. There were three guards outside the shack, all wearing night-vision goggles. They were smoking cigarettes and chatting in hushed voices.

At 11.54 p.m. GMT, moving on silent, winged feet, two SAS commandos inched round from the sides and took out the guards on the left and right with swift blows to their windpipe. Hugh moved in on the third, a much bigger man. The thug screamed in surprise, before he too was laid low by a blow to the chest.

Stepping over him to push the door open, Hugh saw the thug's mouth hanging limply open. It was his old friend, L-O-V-E H-A-T. Hugh gave him a mocking salute, for old times' sake, before he passed through.

Hugh recognised the shack now. It was the abandoned farmhouse where Lucy had hidden out. No sooner had his foot descended than the lights blazed on instantly. The place was kitted out with hidden motion sensors. It was a state-of-the-art system, good enough to fool MI5's satellite intelligence. Armed guards surrounded a man in a homburg hat and dark glasses. At least six of them. He had a DVD camera trained on his face. His finger was poised above a red remote control.

It was Brigham Hope. He laughed, a low growling sound without any suggestion of humour whatsoever. 'Hello. It's Hugh, isn't it?' he said, and glanced at his watch. 'I was expecting some foolish stunt like this. You're five minutes early.'

'Er, yes. Thanks,' said Hugh foolishly. He had never thought about what he'd say when confronting a psychopath.

'In actual fact I was expecting your master, Prime Minister Winston Wright. I suppose he was too cowardly to risk his own neck.'

'Winston couldn't make it,' Hugh replied defensively. 'He was too busy.'

'Too busy to save the world?' the man sneered. 'Or destroy it, should I say?'

He nodded to one of his guards, who turned on the camera and turned off the light. All that could be seen on camera now was the shadow of a man in a homburg hat.

'This is linked up to the Internet and key TV stations. It will be seen around the world live,' Brigham explained.

'Shall we take him out now, sir?' hissed one of the SAS men standing behind him. He knew other commandos were climbing in through a back window. Could they take Brigham, he wondered?

Brigham caught the meaning of the whispering and laughed again. 'No fast moves or I'll press this trigger and Whoosh. The fabulous mines of Paradise. Gone. Now, shut up. I have a message for the world.'

The cameras whirred and Brigham's deep Southern twang rang out:

'PEOPLE OF THE WORLD. ONE OF YOUR LEADERS HAS BEEN VERY, VERY STUPID. HE HAS MOUNTED A SURPRISE ATTACK ON MY ISLAND. WELL, TO BE HONEST IT WASN'T MUCH OF A SURPRISE. A HERD OF ELEPHANTS COULD HAVE BEEN QUIETER. BUT HE PROBABLY THOUGHT HE WAS MOUNTING A SURPRISE ATTACK ON ME.

'WINSTON WRIGHT HAS

DISOBEYED MY ORDERS. HE'S BEEN A RECKLESS JACKASS. BUT WHAT CAN YOU EXPECT? THE BOY IS ONLY TWELVE. IF HE DOESN'T GET HIS BUTT OFF MY LAND, I WILL BLOW THE MINES. YOU ALL KNOW WHAT THAT MEANS. THE LIFE-SAVING ENERGY OF PARADISE. GONE FOR EVER.

'I WILL GIVE HIM TEN MINUTES TO LEAVE THE ISLAND. HE SHOULD NEVER HAVE DREAMED OF TRYING TO OUTWIT ME. NO ONE CAN. MY HEARTBEAT IS LINKED BY MOTOR-NEURONE SENSORS TO THE REMOTE CONTROL. IF YOU TRY TO TAKE ME OUT, THE MINES GO UP IN SMOKE.'

Brigham finished his message and sat in silence for a moment, his hand softly stroking the stubbly hair above his ear. Then he turned to Hugh. 'Winston is finished,' he announced. 'It's time he went back to school.'

CHAPTER THIRTY-THREE

Winston took the call on the jet speeding towards Paradise.

'What the heck you up to?' President Houston hollered. 'You damn fool kid, you're gonna ruin everything.'

'I know what I'm doing, Mr President,' Winston said calmly.

'Geez, it's a mad, mad world. We have a kid in charge of the Brits and he thinks it's fun to blow up the world. Hey, kiddo, I am ordering you. Get out of there. Get out of there right now or I'll reclassify Britain as a rogue state. You'll be –'

Winston hung up and instantly there was another call. 'Weenston, are you crazeee?' it was Giscard De Brée, the President of France. Again

Winston disconnected the phone.

He was ready now. Ready for the biggest gamble of his life.

He made a call himself. To Hugh. When his faithful lieutenant answered his mobile, he asked him to hand it to Brigham Hope. But Brigham Hope refused to take the phone.

So Winston asked his bodyguard to pass on a message. With the fate of the world hanging in the balance, Hugh started to argue.

'Crikey. You can't mean it, Win,' he shouted. Hugh listened for a second longer. 'But what about Lucy and our families and . . .? What about the mines? It's crazy. I can't pass this on. Winston, are you sure? . . . All right. I *will* do as I'm told . . . It probably will be for once, cos I'll never get another chance to do anything. But if I never see . . . OK.'

The madman was watching impatiently. Finally Hugh got off the phone and turned to him. 'Winston says go ahead, Brigham. Go ahead and push the button.'

'What?' Brigham spluttered.

His guards closed nervously around him.

'The Prime Minister of Britain says push the button,' Hugh explained.

Presidents, prime ministers and, the billions watching the showdown live on TV and Internet were stunned.

'Blow up the mines of Paradise,' Brigham said slowly. 'He's off his head.'

'He's calling your bluff,' Hugh explained.

For a second Brigham hesitated.

'It's Winston's decision,' he said. His hand moved to the red button and he pushed it.

A spark raced along the ignition wire buried deep underground. Fsss. It lit the fuse attached to the bombs.

BAMMO. The heavens exploded.

The walls of the hut cracked and the ceiling came down, showering rubble on to Brigham and Hugh. Underfoot, the earth rumbled and rose. The heat melted Hugh's helmet and set off a volley of artillery. The flare could be seen for thousands of miles. Every centimetre of rock and sea lit up an unearthly purple. The sickening smell of bittersweet almonds filled the air. The skies glowed purple, as if it was Judgement Day. Then the heavens opened. A wall of sound rent the surface of the earth. The sound wasn't just loud, it was eardrum-shattering, head-pounding, deafening.

Looking up, Hugh saw the planes. A dozen RAF transport jets with huge speakers growing out of their flanks, like giant mushrooming ears. And from the speakers came music.

Swing low, sweet chariot, coming
For to carry me home.
Swing low, sweet chariot, coming
For to carry me home.
Went to the Doctor, what did I see?
Coming for to carry me home,
A band of angels coming after me,
Coming for to carry me home.

This wasn't the music of harps and heavenly spheres. Its bass notes sounded like the earth splitting.

But the low, deep tones spoke another message to the rocks of Paradise. As the first verse ended, the fire suddenly went out. As swift as a snuffed candle.

One minute Paradise was hell. The next minute the firework display was just a bad memory.

And the island went back to its foggy slumber.

CHAPTER THIRTY-FOUR

'How did you think up that speaker trick?' Hugh looked at his friend, awe-struck. 'It was out of this world!'

The two boys were outside the mine, in the spot where Brigham Hope had been captured. He was safely on an RAF fighter plane now, being flown to a secret interrogation centre. SAS commandos and a battalion of regular troops had neutralised Brigham's mercenaries and secured the mine. They didn't face much opposition. Once the men knew their leader had been captured the fight fizzled out of them.

Winston and Hugh themselves were due to return to England. The PM wanted to be in on the questioning of the captive madman. But first, he told Hugh, he had a small job to do. Winston smiled at Hugh. He felt a wave of affection for his ever-dependable bodyguard. 'You've got to ask me that? The genius who discovered Paradise rock. I think we'll stick with Paradise rock, by the way. The name Hopeite is history.'

Hugh blushed. 'That was an accident. Just a lucky break.'

'I had one too.'

'You had one too?'

'An accident'

'An accident?'

'Hugh,' Winston said, exasperated, 'you must decide whether you're a person or an echo. Yes, I had a lucky accident too. Remember the mobile?'

'The mobile?'

'You're doing it again!'

'Sorry, Win. What about the mobile?'

'It went off in the chem lab. The ringtone put out the fire.'

'But I did that. With my blanket.'

Winston shook his head. 'No. It was the mobile phone ringtone. If it was down to the blanket you, the lab and me would all be cinders.' He paused a moment and added thoughtfully, 'I suppose I have to thank Bob for that. Perhaps its time to promote him from tea boy. I'll make him a press assistant. Or an under-secretary for new technology.'

'Tell me. Tell me everything,' said Hugh greedily.

'It's quite simple really,' Winston explained. 'Paradise rock, like all crystals, has an internal crystalline structure. Every crystal structure has a resonant frequency. By playing a particular sequence of sounds you can reconfigure the internal structure of a crystal and make it inert.'

'Wow!' Hugh's eyes were as big as golf balls. 'So you played calming music to the rocks. And it, like, calmed them down.'

'Exactly.' Winston beamed. '"Swing Low Sweet Chariot" just happened to contain the right note sequence to denature the wonder-fuel at a molecular level. The secret lies in playing the notes in the exact sonic frequency. I think that's perfectly clear?'

'Er, perfectly,' Hugh said. 'Um, the stuff does still work, doesn't it? Paradise rock?'

'Of course. I wouldn't have blown up the mines if I wasn't sure the rocks would still work. We've done tests. The rocks go back to their old crystalline structure once they've been deactivated.'

'Um, right.'

Winston stood up. 'And now I have a very special person to find.'

Hugh knew who it was instantly. 'Lucy.'

Winston nodded. 'She's been extraordinary. I left a camera with her. She's been sending me a running report. Got in places no one else managed.'

The boys trooped past a scene of devastation. Commandos clearing up bullet cases. Fragments of blasted rock. Abandoned guns and the blackened tanks of Brigham Hope's private army. The litter of war turned the marshy green fields of Paradise into a disgusting sight.

They came to the shack which Brigham had turned into his headquarters. Winston walked into the centre of the room and tapped on the floor twice. Then he tapped three times. There was a long pause before the floor began to walk upwards. Hair, indescribably filthy, matted hair, emerged from the trapdoor. Then a skinny little face. It was Lucy. But how she had changed. She looked more skeleton than girl.

'You need some square meals,' said Winston, walking up to her and holding out his arms. 'About a dozen of them to start with.'

Hugh watched them embrace, and it was all he could do to stop the tears coming to his eyes.

'What have you been living on?' Hugh asked.

Lucy reached down into the cellar and brought up a can. 'Baked beans. About half a can a day,' she said with a watery smile. 'I hope I never see another bean again.' She crawled out of the hole and slumped on the floor. Winston poured her some tea from a Thermos flask. After a few minutes the colour began to come back into her cheeks.

'You've helped us so much, Lucy,' Winston said gently.' 'Your footage shocked the world, forced us to take action. What happened to the phone, by the way? I was pretty worried when I couldn't speak to you.'

Lucy shook her head. 'It didn't work.'

Winston frowned. 'It was meant to be a triband phone, so it should operate even at the top of a mountain. It was a stroke of luck that you were hiding right underneath Brigham.'

'If you could call it that –' Lucy sat up very straight. 'The floor in the shack is so rotten I could hear them talking up there. Sometimes I thought Brigham would fall through the floor on me. What a way to go!'

'You're not going anywhere. You made it,' Winston said with a warm smile. 'Lucy, I've got some good news for you.'

Lucy's face lit up: 'My family! They're alive?' she gasped.

'Your mother and brother were held by Brigham's men in the south of the island. They were rescued earlier today by British soldiers. They're shaken. They've had an awful time. But they're alive and well.'

'And Dad?'

Winston shook his head. 'I'm so sorry, Lucy.'

CHAPTER THIRTY-FIVE

'I'm not telling you a thing.' Brigham Hope scowled. He sat in his underpants, his flesh oozing over the edges of the hard metal chair, his hands manacled together. He looked like a baby in an outsize nappy. 'You can beat me up. You can torture me. I still won't tell you a thing.'

'We don't operate like that,' said GQ frostily. 'Your lot may be thugs. We like to think we're civilised.'

GQ and MI5's top interrogator were hard at work on Brigham Hope. The interrogator was a man with a handlebar moustache and sweaty palms. A man you would not want to meet socially.

'We know everything anyway,' added GQ. 'Or almost.'

'Don't expect me to fill in the almost.'

'Why did do you do it? Why risk all when you could have just sold the rock and become insanely rich?'

The man smiled. His eyes were baby blue. 'I'm insane,' he said. 'I'm a madman. I expect the courts will find out I'm a – how do you Brits put it? – a nutcase and let me go on humanitarian grounds.'

'Do you want me to take over?' the interrogator butted in.

'No. I'm handling this,' GQ said. He went on, 'I don't think you're insane. Not at all. I think you know exactly what you're up to.'

Brigham grinned rudely. 'I don't think you know what *you're* up to. Bunch of hopeless losers, that's what I think.'

'I'm not the one manacled to a chair in my underpants,' GQ replied calmly.

Winston and Hugh were watching the scene from behind a two-way mirror. 'Something's wrong with the man.' Winston put his hand over the intercom that communicated with the room and spoke to Hugh in whisper.

'We know that,' Hugh said. 'He's a nutter. And he could do with losing a bit of weight.'

Winston shook his head. 'That's not it.'

The man who had taken the world to the brink of

disaster breathed defiance. But there was also something else. Some other emotion Winston could not quite put his finger on.

Though his plans of world domination were in tatters. Though he was sitting in an interrogation cell in boxer shorts decorated with yellow ducks, Brigham Hope still seemed to feel he had the upper hand.

Were they all being conned?

Suddenly Winston leaned forward and spoke into the intercom that connected with the interrogation room. 'Search him,' he ordered.

GQ turned around and looked straight at the mirror, where he knew Winston must be sitting. 'We already have,' he said, 'several times.'

'Search harder,' Winston said. 'Every last pore. He's hiding something.'

Winston didn't like the way Brigham was stalling. The way he always let a second elapse before he answered a question.

The interrogator picked up a looking glass and began examining the suspect's face with it.

Winston watched every flicker on Brigham's face. His eyes honed in on the way he fiddled with his left ear – a psychological giveaway, if ever he saw one. He leaned forward again. 'I want you to pay special attention to Brigham's ears.'

The interrogator threw a filthy look at the mirror. He seemed to feel that Winston was intruding on his patch. But grumpily he followed orders. When he got to Brigham's left ear the interrogator gave a gasp of surprise. 'There's a scar running all the way round,' he said.

GQ gasped. 'His ear's sewn on. Winston, do you get this?

'Yep,' Winston replied impatiently. 'Take him to surgery. We'll have to find out what's under it.'

Winston glanced at his watch. Under European law they could hold a suspect for twenty-four hours without charge – they had eight hours left. 'Come on, get a move on.'

'You lunatics, this is against my human rights,' Brigham wailed. But it was no good. The guards were called and Brigham Hope was rushed in an ambulance to MI5's surgical wing.

It was a forty-five mile drive and Brigham scream-ed and swore and spat the whole way. Eventually he had to be given a sedative. By the time they got to the state-of-the-art operating theatre Brigham was sleeping like a baby on Calpol. The operation was to be conducted by one of Britain's top surgeons.

Winston, Hugh and GQ watched from the sidelines, dressed from head to toe in surgical gowns and masks.

'Knife,' the surgeon said.

A nurse handed him a blade that glittered dangerously in the bright lights of the operating theatre.

'I hope you're not going to cut it off,' Hugh blurted out. 'I'm sorry, but it's gross.'

'Goodness, no.' The surgeon smiled. 'His ear is held on by tiny stitches. I'm going to use this blade to unpick them. Don't worry, he won't feel a thing. Though I must warn you there is a risk of bleeding.'

Hugh was very pale. Winston nodded, feeling more queasy than he would have liked to admit.

The ear was unpicked in less than ten minutes. The stitches were of the finest nylon. When they were undone, white bone and little whorls of pink flesh that looked like shelled prawns were exposed. And nestling in the middle of the flesh and bone was something entirely non-organic in origin. A round plastic box, no bigger than the tip of a baby's finger, attached to a small wire. One of the smallest intercoms Winston had ever seen.

So his hunch was right. Brigham Hope was far from being the genius behind the capture of Paradise Island. In fact he was just another actor.

Winston leaned over the intercom with a confident smile. 'Finally I get to talk to the man who pulls the strings.'

Nothing was more unexpected than the laughter which burst through the intercom like a series of silvery bubbles. They caused the robed surgeons, spooks and nurses crammed into the operating room to freeze like statues. 'You silly old sexist,' a girlish voice trilled. 'Whatever makes you think I'm a man?'

Winston took a moment to collect his wits. 'It's probably my conditioning. I was unlucky enough to go to an all-boys school.'

'Yeah, well, I'm a chick and I'm in charge. You Brits may live in the past. Us Yanks, we're in the twenty-first century.'

'Who are you?' Winston asked the ear.

'I'm Brigham Hope,' the female trilled playfully. 'Or then again, maybe I'm not.'

Winston had a moment of pure inspiration. 'I'm speaking to Hope Brigham, am I not? You're Miss Speller, South Moines, winner with one hundred per cent correct answers. You've certainly come a long way from South Moines, Hope.'

'Oh, that stupid spelling bee. You know about that!

Well, school was a drag, ya know. I couldn't wait to move on.'

'I must confess I often felt the same way,' Winston said. 'People told me I was in too much of a hurry.'

'Too right, Winston Wright. I do believe this is the beginning of a beautiful friendship.' Hope's laughter resounded round the operating theatre again.

Winston seized his chance. 'I've got to tell you, Hope, I've never been one for the pen-pal thing. Let's meet. Get to know one another.'

'You wanna *meet* me?'

'I've got to.'

'Why?'

'I think we'd like each other.'

'Sorry. I don't do face-time.'

'Make an exception for me.'

There was a long, long silence. And then finally Hope Brigham spoke. 'All right,' she said. 'I admit it, I'm curious. We'll meet. My guys will send you the details. But I'm warning you, just you. No sats, no back-up, no nothing.'

'Um, I'll have to bring my driver, Hugh Ray-Chaudhary. You see, I'm not old enough to have a licence.'

The voice sighed. 'All right. But you're both to

wear dark glasses. And he's to keep his back to me at all times. I don't want him *looking* at me.'

'You've got a deal,' Winston said.

CHAPTER THIRTY-SIX

Red rock stretched as far as the eye could see, red rock and yellow sand. It soared up into the sky in dizzy-making cliffs which could have been hewn out of gigantic sides of sun-dried beef.

Winston and Hugh had been dropped by helicopter in Batopilas and in strict secrecy had trekked their exhausted way here – the heart of Mexico's Copper Canyon. The scenary was amazing, but Winston scarcely noticed. His gaze was drawn, as if by a magnet, to Hope.

She was so pale she was almost see-through. White-blonde hair hung down to her waist and her skin was the colour of snow. Her mouth and features were bleached out, as if someone had scribbled over her face with white crayons. Hope looked at Winston with pale, unreadable eyes. 'So, we meet at last.'

Winston couldn't stop staring at her. She was thirteen, fourteen at the most. There was something elfin about her ears, her pale eyes. She was the strangest creature he had ever seen. She reminded him of someone, but at the moment he couldn't think who. He walked forward and held out his hand for a shake, but the girl shrank back.

'I don't do touching,' she said. 'Keep at last ten paces away from me.'

'As you wish.' Winston backed off.

'I've come to tell you that you haven't won. The game's just begun.'

'I never thought I had,' Winston replied.

'Paradise is mine. You've taken it from me by force but I'll win it back through the courts. Sir Giles signed it over to me.'

'You're in with a chance. A fair chance,' Winston admitted. 'Tell me, Hope. What's in it for you? What do you really want?'

'I thought I made it quite clear. I want to get away. I'm sick of it all. Maybe when you're my age you'll understand what it's like to be sick of life.'

'How old are you?'

'I don't do personal information. Anyway, age

isn't temporal, it's a mental thing.'

'And your friends and family, how do they feel?'

The girl snorted. 'I got none. Well, none that I care about. They're all sheep. Can't think for themselves, can't act for themselves. They bore me to tears. You've met my dad.'

'What?' Then enlightenment dawned on Winston. 'That was your dad. I thought he was just another actor.'

'Whatever.' The girl flicked her hair back with a languid hand.

'And you did that to him? The ear?'

'I told you, he couldn't think for himself. He kept getting stuff wrong. Useless pig. That way I was inside his head, whenever he needed me.'

Winston stared curiously at the girl through his dark glasses. What a brain. 'How long have you been in, um, *business* for yourself?'

'Couple of years. But, hey, I've always been precocious.'

'So have I.' Winston smiled.

For the first time a flicker of amusement crossed the girl's face. 'Why do you think I agreed to meet you?'

At that moment Hugh turned round and the girl scowled.

'Get your goon to turn round, else I'll have to have

him whacked. I wouldn't like that. I hate needless suffering.' She scowled.

Hastily Hugh turned his back on the pair again. And Winston turned on his most charming smile. It wasn't hard, as he found he truly wanted to win over this enigmatic creature. 'The funny thing is, Hope, you've got so much to live for. You're the most brilliant person I've ever met. You could do so much for this planet.'

A spot of red appeared on the chalky cheeks. 'With the great unwashed.'

'People aren't so bad. They could learn from you. You're so much sharper than anyone else I've met.'

'People aren't willing to learn. They don't listen.'

'I think they would listen to you.'

'People get on my nerves. I want my own space now.' The girl began to turn her back on Winston. Clearly the audience with Hope Brigham was over.

'Hope,' Winston called.

She turned round.

'One thing. Could I have the photos of Sir Giles? I think they've served their purpose.'

Hope laughed.

'They can't be of any further use. Lushington is in a rest home now. He's finished.'

'They amuse me.'

'I think Sir Giles has suffered enough,' Winston said quietly. 'You told me you hated unnecessary suffering.'

'Whatever. Quit bugging me. We've all got skeletons in our cupboard.'

'I've got none. Apart from my mother's habit of calling me Winnie.'

Just for a moment a real grin broke through Hope's body armour. 'You might have skeletons you're not aware of.'

Something tinkled at Winston's feet. He looked down. It was a bunch of keys. He bent to pick them up, straightened himself and opened his mouth to thank the girl. But she'd gone. Winston looked to his right. There was nothing there but a scattering of orange rocks. To his left, a large green cactus. Hope had dematerialised into the emptiness of the desert. Vanished as totally as if she had never been there.

CHAPTER THIRTY-SEVEN

Hugh put the key in locker 225. Lying inside was a brown-paper envelope. He took the envelope out and put it in his dispatch bag. Then he sauntered outside Victoria station, where his bike was parked against a railing. The bike, a Harley Triumph, was a thank-you present from Winston. Going at the kind of break-neck speeds that Winston had warned him against, Hugh was at Number Ten in ten. Minutes that is.

Winston was at his desk, red boxes full of papers in front of him. He took the envelope from Hugh and glanced inside.

'Bad?' asked Hugh.

'Very. I'm afraid,' Winston replied. 'Want a look?'

Hugh eagerly held out his hand for the photos of Sir Giles Lushington that Hope Brigham had used for blackmail. He looked at them in stunned silence for a minute. Then let out a giggle. 'I'd say they're more silly than bad,' he smirked.

'Whatever,' Winston said 'He's done for . . . We need to get these pics sent to this address.' He wrote an address on a scrap of paper and gave it to Hugh. 'Could you please take them to the porter downstairs?'

For twenty-four hours Winston's political career – and more importantly the future of the world – hung in the balance. True, British troops now controlled Paradise. And many of the confused boat people had started to return to their homes. And there was more good news. The mines of the island were producing their first hauls of the fabulous purple crystal.

But the fate of the crystal hung in the balance. Sir Giles had definitely signed over governorship of the island to the Paradise International Corporation, President Hope Brigham. And the document was legally valid and binding. And many of the residents of Paradise Island had signed over their property to Hope's company.

Meanwhile Winston's own reputation with the voters of Britain tottered. He had shown real leadership in capturing Paradise. And his calming music scam had worked a treat. But he had so nearly got the mines blown to smithereens. People couldn't forget how close to the wire he'd walked. Was it his age that made him so reckless, the newspapers wondered?

On Friday the Law Lords of Europe spoke. They had pored over the legal documents relating to Paradise Island till their eyes watered. They had also considered the photos of Sir Giles for twenty-four hours (longer than strictly necessary – but even Law Lords like a laugh).

. . . Sir Giles was of 'unsound mind' when he signed Paradise over to Hope Brigham. The paperwork is invalid, especially in relation to subsection 448, clause 52. The mines of the island have been saved from Hope Brigham . . .

The world exploded with joy and John Minor – who had been completely cleared, along with the other victims of the faked scandals – was one of the first to join the party.

Somewhere, Hope Brigham probably gnashed her pearly-whites at the completeness of Winston's victory. The rest of the world didn't care. An international holiday was declared. There were carnivals in Brazil, fiestas in Spain, hoedowns in the USA, melas in India, barbies in Australia – the biggest parties the world had ever seen.

In London the Queen arrived in her gold and black coach pulled by snow-white horses to open Parliament.

Winston's mum, Shirley, and sister, Gemma, were watching the scene from the front of the huge crowd as Winston, accompanied by his bodyguard, Hugh, walked out of Parliament to meet Her Majesty. His mum's heart swelled with pride, even as a burly grandmother tried to elbow her out of the way with her handbag. Her Winnie, chatting to the Queen.

The Queen patted Winston on the hand affection-ately. 'You're very clever, my boy,' she piped up. 'Got us out of a tight hole.'

'Thanks, Your Majesty.'

The Queen's blue eyes twinkled at the shortest Prime Minister who had ever led one of her governments. She had a feeling she was going to get on famously with this one.

'Call me Liz,' the Queen said, beaming.